CHARMER

KINGS OF THE EAST #11

CHARITY PARKERSON

PUNK & SISSY PUBLICATIONS

COPYRIGHT

poses if credit is given to the copyright holder. Your support of the author's rights is appreciated. Any resemblances to person(s) living or dead, is completely coincidental. All items contained within this novel are products of the author's imagination.

—Warning: This book is intended for readers over the age of 18. Some of my books contain allusions to past abuse and trauma. I try to have nothing triggering on page and treat every situation with care.

Editor: BZ Hercules & Consultants

ISBN: 978-1-959576-02-0

CONTENTS

AUTHOR NOTE

THIS SERIES IS DARKER than my usual writing. If you need a list of potential triggers, you can skip to the end of this book and find a list after the About Author page. You can also visit my website at charityparkerson.com/kings-of-the-east, if you'd prefer.

INTRODUCTION

*A DOCTOR CATERING TO **the most danger-
ous men in the world meets a charming
nobody. Neither wants to believe the other is what they seem. They're both wrong.***

As one of Zander Kapra's team and a
survivor of the cause, Corey helps by
putting his medical degree to good use.
He goes wherever he's needed to keep
the family safe. Sometimes, that means
patching up assassins and helping dis-
pose of evidence. Mostly, it's helping the
victims after their rescue. It's a calling.
He'll never stop. Now, there's this guy
who won't stop trying to win him, and

Corey doesn't know what to think. Mostly, he thinks Rhett is full of it.

Meeting Corey was the most random moment of Rhett's life. One second, he was chatting with a friend. The next, Rhett was staring into the sweetest face he's ever seen. Corey keeps trying to make him go away. Rhett can't do that. He's hooked. Now all he has to do is convince Corey to keep him. How hard could it be?

Charmer is the eleventh book in Charity Parkerson's Kings of the East series where assassins, crime lords, and mafia bosses run the world. These books are best when read in order.

CHAPTER ONE

WITH A HOT COFFEE in one hand and a tall blond holding his other, Corey walked down the street in the neighborhood where he always got his coffee. His legs felt wooden. Like a marionette on a string, he let Rhett drag him along. Corey didn't understand what had happened. One second, he had stepped inside a bakery to say hello to his friend, Jordan. The next, Jordan introduced him to Rhett. Then Rhett had grabbed his arm and hauled him out of the bakery, and down the street for an unwanted coffee date. Corey had been along for the ride ever since. It was all so stupid.

In theory, he possessed the ability to walk away. Not only was he a grown man, but he was also a very capable one. He was a doctor and hard as steel on the inside. Yet—somehow—this over-the-top bubbly cream puff, who seemed like he had a head full of air, kept Corey hostage with a nonstop flow of words. Corey was trapped somewhere between the need to run for his life and horrified fascination. He didn't know how to make it stop.

"And then I went to college to become a teacher but ended up majoring in physical education."

"Yeah. That's a teacher."

Rhett obviously didn't care about the dead note in Corey's tone; he just kept going. "I know, right?" Rhett laughed.

"How did I end up in charge of over a hundred kids every day?"

"That's a lot of kids."

If Rhett heard the disinterest in Corey's voice, he didn't acknowledge it. "Well, it's closer to two hundred. We have eight class periods a day. Well, one of them is a planning period, but still. In my seven classes where I have students, I have between twenty and twenty-five students in each class. Actually, in a few, it's almost thirty. So that's…" Rhett stared into the distance.

"Between one hundred and forty and two hundred and ten students."

Rhett flashed him a bright smile. "Wow. You did that in your head? You're smart. What do you do for a living?"

Corey saw his chance. Rhett had actually paused speaking for more than five seconds. He could run for it. Fuck. Rhett was a gym teacher. He could probably run fast. Corey likely wouldn't get away. He could already picture Rhett chasing after him, still talking while completely oblivious to the fact that he chased Corey. Best he just answered. "I'm a doctor."

Somehow, Rhett's smile got even brighter. "That's amazing." He could light a whole town with his charisma. Corey was exhausted just by being in his company. "Your parents are probably so proud."

"They're dead." Corey looked at his watch. "I have house calls to make. This has been... something, but I have to go."

Rhett didn't look fazed. "That's fine. I'll walk you to your car so you can give me your number."

Corey bit back a sigh. "You don't have to do that. I'm parked way back in the coffee shop parking lot."

"Nonsense." While still clinging to Corey's hand, Rhett turned and headed back toward the coffee shop. "I couldn't possibly leave someone as gorgeous as you to make the walk alone. Someone might try to abduct you."

"I've killed enough people. I'm sure I can take care of myself."

Rhett laughed. "Was that a doctor joke I just heard? You're funny."

Corey gave up and let Rhett have his way. He wasn't sure if Rhett was dumb or manipulative. Either way, Corey's will obviously wasn't as strong as Rhett's malfunction.

Rhett bounced as they neared the parking lot where Corey had left his car. "Which of these cars is yours?"

Corey motioned toward a nondescript gray SUV. He purposely tried not to stand out anywhere he went. "That one."

Rhett bounced on his toes again, making Corey wonder if he had some medical condition that forced him to act on his every impulse. "Wow. It really was fate for us to meet. I'm the blue Bronco next to you."

The hair rose on the back of Corey's neck. He didn't believe in coincidences. "That's an expensive vehicle for a teacher."

Rhett blushed, fascinating Corey. He didn't strike Corey as the type to be embarrassed by anything. "Um. Yeah." He rubbed the back of his neck. "I do some side hustling." Rhett didn't elaborate.

Corey didn't ask. "Okay. Well. I have to run."

"Whoa. Hold up." Rhett set his coffee cup on the hood of Corey's vehicle and pulled a Sharpie from his back pocket.

"You keep a Sharpie in your pocket?"

Rhett pulled the cap off with his teeth and smiled around it as he stole Corey's cup and wrote his number on it. He waited until the marker was back in his pocket before responding. "I'm a teacher. There's always pens and what-not in my pockets."

"It's Sunday."

Rhett winked.

While Corey tried recovering from the odd sensation the wink caused in his chest, Rhett shot forward and pressed his lips to Corey's. It was over as fast as it happened.

Rhett grabbed his cup and walked away. "It was nice meeting you, Corey," he said over his shoulder, "and don't forget to call me."

Corey stared at Rhett's retreating form. He moved with so much confidence; it was hard not to watch. His gray t-shirt stretched across sexy wide shoulders and protested against his large biceps. He wore his jeans a bit baggy, but that detail did nothing to hide an exquisite ass. Nothing good came from people like Rhett. Corey shook his head—breaking the trance. Before he climbed behind the wheel, he pulled his phone from his pocket. He found his friend Ransom's number and waited until his phone connected with the Bluetooth in his car before hitting the call icon. The sound of ringing filled the vehicle. Ransom answered just as Corey had almost given up hope.

"Hello?"

"Hey, Ransom. It's Corey. I need you to look into someone for me."

The sound of shuffling came through the speakers, as if Ransom changed ears. "Okay. That's not a problem. I'm ready. What's the name?"

"All I have is a first name and a phone number."

"That's all I need."

Corey had suspected as much. "Good. Rhett. His number is 555-9007."

A moment of silence met his request. Corey swore he felt Ransom's confusion even before he spoke. "That's weird."

An eerie feeling overcame Corey. He had known there was something off about Rhett. No one could be as puppy-like as Rhett pretended to be. "What is it?"

"I've already investigated Rhett for Timofey."

That made sense now that Corey thought about it. Timofey wouldn't allow just anyone to be friends with his husband, Jordan. "What did you learn?"

"Nothing," Ransom said without missing a beat. "He's clean. Well, relatively speaking."

"What do you mean?"

Ransom paused again before he answered, as if didn't want to say. "It's a bit of a conflict of interest for me, really. He's a member of a club my husband manages and bartends, Leather Bait. It's a fetish club and he wouldn't be happy if he knew I was outing their clients."

Corey didn't give a fuck about anyone's feelings. This was about his safety. "I wouldn't ask if this wasn't important."

"I'll send you his file, but seriously. Rhett is harmless. He's just a normal guy."

"Still."

"All right," Ransom said, sounding re-signed. "Give me a few and I'll send you an encrypted email."

Corey smiled. He liked Ransom. It wasn't beyond his notice that Ransom didn't have to help him. "I appreciate it. Seriously. Send me a bill for your time. I get you didn't have to help me."

"It's fine. Timofey already paid me for the job." He hesitated before saying more. "Plus, I agree. It's odd for his name to come up twice. If you spot something I didn't, let me know. As I said, he's someone who has access to my husband. If he's more than he seems and I need to handle this, I will."

Even though Ransom couldn't see him, Corey made a dismissive motion. "Don't worry. I just want a peek at his file. If Timofey didn't kill him, I can't imagine there's anything to worry about. This is more about my peace of mind than anything else."

"All right, then. The file should be in your inbox now."

Corey smiled. "Thank you."

"It's no problem. Talk to you soon."

"Sure thing." Corey disconnected the call and pulled from the parking lot. He hadn't been lying. There were patients waiting for him today, but he would make time to figure out Rhett's agenda. There was no way Corey had caught his eye. Corey purposely didn't catch eyes. He much preferred being invisible. Rhett had an agenda. Corey would figure it out and then he would take care of the problem. No one would make an idiot of him. Corey's was no one's toy. Not anymore.

As much as Rhett had wanted to beg Corey for his number, Rhett had to hope Corey called instead. He knew people thought he was just a clueless lump, but he had been a teacher for a long time. Rhett was observant and knew how to read people. Corey didn't want to be interested in Rhett for whatever reason, but he was, and he would call. Rhett was fully aware of his faults. He knew he could be overwhelming, but he also knew his worth, and Corey looked like a smart guy.

"Hey, Mr. Porter."

Rhett turned at the sound of his name. One of last year's students headed his way with what looked to be her dad in tow.

"I thought that was you. How are you?"

A bright smile stretched Rhett's lips. He loved being a teacher. It never bothered him to run into students outside of school. "Terry. Hey. I'm good. How was your summer break?"

Terry smiled. "It was great. We spent three weeks on vacation before school started back."

"Really? Where did you go?"

"The mountains. I can't remember the name of the town." She glanced her father's way.

He jumped in. "Gatlinburg." He held out his hand for Rhett to shake. "I'm Marshall, Terry's dad. It's nice to meet you."

Rhett shifted his coffee cup from one hand to the other and shook Marshall's hand. "Rhett Porter. I was your daughter's PE teacher last year."

"I've heard the name. Terry told me how you stopped that awful group of girls from bullying her."

Rhett made a dismissive motion. "It comes with the job."

Marshall shook his head. "Apparently, it doesn't. A lot of the other teachers ignored the problem. I appreciate you stepping up the way you did."

Rhett nodded. As he said, it was part of the job, but he wouldn't keep arguing. He still had errands to run. "It was nice meeting you." His gaze shifted Terry's way. "And it was good running into you. Good luck this year and enjoy it. Your senior year goes by too fast, and you'll miss it someday."

Terry laughed.

Marshall's gaze continued boring into Rhett in a way that wasn't entirely comfortable. "I feel like I've seen you before somewhere. It's driving me crazy."

Rhett did his best to keep smiling. "I just have one of those faces."

After a moment, Marshall shook head and smiled. "We live in the same town, and you teach at my kid's school. I'm sure we've passed each other a dozen times."

"That's probably it."

After a few more minutes of untangling himself, Rhett walked away with Corey eclipsing every other thought again. He hoped Corey called. That sweet smile and those sexy blue eyes weren't easy to shake. He was a doctor. That was hot. Rhett wanted to know him better. He would call. Rhett couldn't accept any other outcome.

CHAPTER TWO

COREY WASN'T THE TYPE to make up reasons to a see a patient, especially without an appointment. The Butcher also wasn't the type of man a person dropped in on unexpectedly. Today, Corey made an exception. Luckily, for the sake of his life, Corey heard them before ringing the doorbell.

"That's it, beautiful. Damn. Touching you never gets old."

Corey froze. The porch wrapped around the house. It was obvious they were either outside or had a window open. Corey didn't dare make a sound. He couldn't walk into this situation.

A whimper cut through the air.

Corey took a step back.

An evil-sounding chuckle followed the whimper.

Corey stopped moving again. He wasn't as sure any longer that the whimper had been one of pleasure. He walked softly, silently following the sound. Corey quickly peeked around the corner of the house. That split second seared itself into Corey's brain as he turned away and headed back for his car. He didn't dare make a single noise and give himself away. Once he was back behind the wheel of his car, Corey didn't move. He stared at nothing. The image of Jordan on Timofey's lap played through his head. He couldn't stop seeing Timofey holding Jordan's throat while his other hand played inside Jordan's shorts. It wasn't the act that punched Corey in the chest. Timofey had moved on from his past. Lately, it felt like everyone had while Corey sat still, incapable of forgetting. The anger and the trauma of his childhood kept him frozen all hours of the day. He hated feeling this way.

Corey dug his cellphone from the pocket of his doctor's coat. He didn't have to hunt for the information Ransom had sent him. It lived in his head rent-free already. Rhett's side hustle was a home-based personal porn subscription. Corey hadn't resisted subscribing immediately. He logged in and scrolled through the video selection. Corey didn't open any of them. He hadn't found the courage for that yet. It didn't matter no one would ever know. Corey would know he had sexualized Rhett. Instead, he found a video with a cover image that showed Rhett's face. He really was beautiful. Corey didn't understand why he kept obsessing over this. Without thinking, he clicked the video. The still shot of Rhett changed.

"Hey, subscribers—"

A knock landed on his window, scaring him so much, he tossed the phone. He blinked like an owl at the sight of Timofey standing at his driver's side window. The sound of Rhett's voice still filled the car. Corey scrambled for the phone. He tried hiding the screen while killing the video. Heat crawled up his face as he started the car to roll down the window. As his phone connected to the Bluetooth, Rhett's voice came through the speakers. Corey quickly turned off the radio. His face felt hot enough to fry an egg.

"Um. Timofey. Hey. How are you?"

"Why are you sitting in the driveway?"

Corey took a steadying breath. "Sorry. I was nearby and decided to stop in to do a follow-up check of your wound. Then a patient called, and I got sidetracked. How are you?" He recognized he had already asked that, but Timofey hadn't answered. Timofey had been stabbed a few weeks back, and Corey had stitched the wound. The stitches had since been removed, but Corey had only stopped by to ask a few questions about Rhett on the sly. Now he felt too dumb to ask anything and he had to ride this lie out to the very end.

Timofey's eerie light blue gaze moved over Corey's face. "I'm good. You can check how things are progressing if you'd like."

With a nod, Corey stepped from his SUV. Timofey wasn't wearing a shirt. In fact, he was in swim trunks. Corey wondered if he had caught them headed to the beach. Obviously, they had gotten sidetracked, but that wasn't Corey's business. He fell back on his calling to save him. The way he always did. Corey probed at the healing wound. It looked good.

"Everything looks great. It'll probably be one heck of a scar, but it looks like Jordan has been taking great care of you."

"He never fails me."

Corey smiled at Timofey's matter-of-fact tone. "I'm happy for you." As the words left him, Corey realized they were true. "You deserve this new start." He didn't meet Timofey's stare as he made the claim. It wasn't personal. Making eye contact was uncomfortable for him. He had an irrational fear of being seen. If anyone looked too closely, they might know he was a mess.

"Thank you. Jordan tells me you were practically dragged down the street by Charisma Chad yesterday."

Corey's eyebrows rose.

Timofey shook his head. "Rhett."

An unexpected laugh burst from Corey. It was a good description. "Yeah. He roped me into coffee. I survived. Barely."

A bright smile lit Timofey's face. Corey blinked. He had never seen Timofey smile. Jordan had changed him. It was nice.

"He's harmless."

"So everyone keeps telling me," Corey said. He sounded dry, even to his ears.

Timofey squeezed his shoulder.

Corey fought not to flinch.

Timofey didn't seem to notice. "Trust me. I vetted the guy from every possible angle. He doesn't have any skeletons."

"Unless you count the porn site." The words fell from Corey's lips before he could stop them.

Timofey's eyebrows tried crawling to his hairline. He looked as if he fought a smile. "I see."

"What do you see?"

"You like him. That's good. He's a good fit for you."

Corey fought a blush. "No one is a good fit for me, but thanks for the insight."

For a moment, Timofey didn't respond. Finally, he took a step back, as if ready to get back to his husband. "I'll stay out of it. It was good seeing you."

Corey immediately felt like shit. He hated when he felt people trying to connect with him and he just couldn't click. "I'll set you free from my care. If you need to return to work, you have my blessing." Corey didn't wait for a response before climbing behind the wheel again. Timofey walked away while Corey found his phone again and killed the video. He purposefully kept his gaze averted from what Rhett did on the screen. With his heart in his throat, Corey couldn't make himself leave the driveway. He gave in to temptation and clicked on Rhett's contact information. Before he lost his nerve, he sent Rhett a text.

Corey: *This is Corey. I forgot to say thank you for the coffee yesterday.*

There. It was done. The text meant nothing. He never had to respond, even if Rhett did. But Corey had stepped outside his comfort zone and that was something to be proud of doing. He had made a stride. Fuck his life.

When the phone buzzed on the table beside his lounge chair, Rhett almost ignored it. His hands were covered in tanning oil. He used that detail as an excuse for the way he juggled the phone and nearly dropped the device when he saw Corey's text. A smile tugged at the corners of his mouth as he read. Then he saved Corey's number so he wouldn't lose it. He couldn't take any chances. Corey was a runner.

Rhett couldn't stop smiling. Corey had sent the most begrudging text Rhett had ever seen, but he had still texted Rhett. That was a win in Rhett's book.

Rhett didn't bother texting him back. He called. Rhett held back a snicker as he listened to the phone ring. He swore he felt Corey panicking and trying to decide whether he should answer.

It rang five times before Corey's voice came through the line. "Dr. A."

"Mhmm. What does the A stand for?"

"Annoyed. I prefer texting."

This time, Rhett couldn't fight his laughter. Even to his ears, his chuckle sounded wicked. "I figured as much. That's why I called."

Silence met his statement.

Rhett pressed on. "What are you doing right now?"

"Sitting in a patient's driveway, talking to you."

"It's a hundred degrees outside. My apartment keeps the pool open year-round. Come enjoy it with me."

"I'm working." Not only did Corey shoot him down fast, but he also did so with zero interest in his voice.

Rhett couldn't hide how discouraged he felt over Corey's lack of responsiveness to his flirting. "Oh. Okay. Maybe some other time."

Silence dragged on between them while Rhett's disappointment grew. Corey genuinely didn't seem interested.

"Well, I guess I should let you get back to work."

Corey cleared his throat. "Maybe, if you're not busy tomorrow after school, we could get coffee again."

Confidence filled Rhett's chest. Honestly, his faith in himself never went away for long, but Corey kept him on his toes. "I'd love that. Same place. About four?"

"Yeah. I can do that."

Giddiness had Rhett ready to run laps around the pool. "Good. I thought about your smile all night last night. You didn't show it enough yesterday. Maybe I can remedy that tomorrow."

"Okay."

Rhett bit his bottom lip to stop himself from laughing at Corey's monotone response. It seemed he truly intended to make Rhett work for every inch of progress he made. "I'll see you tomorrow, sexy."

Corey released a tired-sounding sigh and disconnected their call without saying goodbye. For some reason Rhett couldn't explain, that made him laugh.

He opened his emails, so he wasn't staring at nothing while smiling like an idiot. There was a message request from the site hosting his videos. The rerouted messages from fans usually went straight in the trash after he skimmed them. They usually fell into two categories: thirsty descriptions of what they would do to Rhett's body or fiery speeches about how he would burn in hell. Rhett had no desire to read either.

His smile fell as his gaze moved over the latest email.

Mr. Porter,

First off, he used a fake name for his videos. Secondly, no one called him that but students.

I finally remembered where I had seen you before. I've been subscribed to your channel for almost two years now. It never occurred to me we lived in the same town. Much less

*that you'd be one of my daughter's teach-
ers. Hopefully, this isn't one of those "do not
respond" email addresses that go nowhere.
Now that I know who you are and where you
live, may I take you to dinner? My number is
below.*

A huge fan,

Marshall

The air left Rhett's lungs. It had always been one of his biggest fears that
a student would find out his secret. A
parent was just as bad. He could lose
his job. Rhett loved teaching. It was
his passion, but it didn't pay enough
for him to support himself. He was already up against a hate-filled political
agenda in his profession. All it would
take was for the wrong person to catch
wind of his second job. He didn't know
what to do. Obviously, he couldn't respond. Not only was he not interested,

but Marshall could also ruin his career. Since Marshall gave him an out with the "do not respond" thing, Rhett would take it. He would pretend he didn't see the message. Hopefully, Marshall would take the hint and the worst that happened would be him losing a subscriber. Fuck. He didn't need this stress. It only fed his desire to move somewhere new. But he had just met someone great, and Rhett wanted to pursue that. He would put Marshall's message out of his mind for now. Terry wasn't in his class any longer. Hopefully, he had no reason to worry. Plus, Rhett had an adorable doctor to chase. That made everything look brighter.

CHAPTER THREE

NORMALLY, RHETT DIDN'T GET nervous about dates, especially for onc as simple as coffee. He was pretty self-sufficient. Not to mention, Rhett doubted anyone would date him seriously while he made porn on the side. It didn't matter all his videos were of him alone. People didn't usually feel secure in a relationship with him. Something about today was different, though. He was oddly anxious about meeting Corey again. Truthfully, Corey was a bit out of his league. His mom would absolutely shit herself with joy if he brought home a doctor, especially since she had given up hope of him ever dating anyone seriously enough to introduce them to her.

As he stepped inside the coffee shop, he spotted Corey immediately. With a cup between his hands, Corey sat in a booth and stared at nothing. He was such a still person. Reserved. Rhett bet good money Corey was one of those who exploded into the kinkiest person alive once he dropped his guard. He desperately wanted to find out. If Corey noticed him, he didn't show it. Rhett took his time. He ordered his coffee and then watched Corey while he waited. Rhett took a steadying breath. Corey was gorgeous. He practically bled privilege and Rhett found that incredibly hot for reasons he couldn't explain.

CHARMER

The moment his order was ready, Rhett moved to join Corey. "Hello, beautiful. I wasn't sure you'd actually show."

Corey didn't smile, nor did he meet Rhett's stare directly. "Why? I asked you. It doesn't make sense for me not to show."

Rhett slid into the booth across from Corey and waited until Corey's gaze moved his way before he responded. "You don't seem like you like me very much. I didn't know if you'd bother with me again."

"I like you just fine."

A smile snapped to Rhett's face at the matter-of-fact tone. "I like you better than fine."

Corey's face screwed up in confusion. "Why? You don't know me."

"I'd like to. Plus, I've had plenty of people I've disliked without really knowing them over the years. I don't see why I can't like someone before I know them."

Corey's confusion cleared a hair, but he didn't completely go back to his usual cool state. "I suppose that's fair."

They both sipped their coffee.

Corey toyed with his cup. "So, how was your day at school?"

Rhett smiled at Corey's choice of wording, as if Rhett had been one of the kids getting an education. "It was good. I mean, it's still the first of the year. Things are always hectic for the first couple of months. I'm still learning kids' names and classes are constantly getting rearranged. Otherwise, it was a typical day. What about you? How did your day go?"

Corey shrugged. "I volunteer at a free clinic on Tuesdays, so it was a busy one."

"That's amazing." Every new detail Rhett learned about Corey made him like the guy a little more. He wanted more. "What do you do for fun?"

For a moment, Corey looked confused by the question, as if the idea of fun was out of his realm. "Um, I'm pretty boring, honestly." Before Rhett argued, Corey made a dismissive motion. "Maybe boring isn't the right description. I'm too busy to do a lot of extracurricular things. My job requires a ton of travel, so maybe... traveling?"

Rhett swallowed a laugh. Corey was fucking adorable. "What kind of doctor travels a lot for work?"

"The kind with elite clientele all over the world."

Corey got farther out of Rhett's league by the second, but they were both still there. Rhett hadn't lost hope. "Really? That's amazing. You must be great at your job. I'd think rich people would want some old dude with forty years' experience under his belt."

The confusion was back. "Was that an insult?"

"Not at all." Rhett rushed to fix his mistake. "It was a compliment. You must be the best."

"Oh." Corey didn't sound one way or the other about Rhett's attempt at smoothing things over. "I suppose I'm adequate."

Rhett shook his head. Corey was an odd one. Rhett didn't know how to crack his shell. "I can't decide if you're being modest or if you hate talking about yourself."

Corey didn't respond right away. Finally, he smiled and took Rhett's breath. "Both."

The fact that Corey seemed to be warming up to him wasn't lost on Rhett. He needed to fan the flames. "We can talk about me if you'd like. I'm not the least bit modest."

Corey's smile grew. "I get that impression about you." His smile faltered. "Honestly, I do have one question that's been bothering me. How did you meet Jordan? Was he one of your students?"

Rhett blushed. "Hmm. Well. No. We met at a wedding. He had a glass of champagne in his hand, so I thought he had to be at least twenty-one. I knew he looked young, but hell. The older I get, the less I'm able to judge age. I didn't find out until we grabbed coffee one day that he's only nineteen. Thankfully, he grew up in the country and went to a rural county school. It would've been really embarrassing if he had been a former student I didn't remember or whatever."

Corey pulled a face. "I didn't want to bring up the age difference or anything, but yeah. That would've been bad. There are a lot of predators out there."

Rhett blinked. He was about fifty percent sure Corey had just called him a pedo. "Wow."

Corey backtracked. Sort of. He didn't sound guilty at all, really. "I'm just saying, it isn't uncommon amongst your profession and Jordan is nearly half your age."

Rhett took a steadying breath. He wasn't one to lose his temper. "I'm not here with Jordan, am I? Or do you consider yourself too young for me too? You know, I've been nothing but nice to you. I thought you just had a tough shell or something, but no. That's not it. You're just not very nice."

"Rhett, I—"

"Thank you for asking me out," Rhett said, talking over the top of Corey. "Even though I'm pretty sure you only did so you could put me in place. I won't bother you again." Rhett grabbed his coffee and headed for the door. He didn't look back. Despite the cruelty of Corey's words, Rhett hated walking away. He wasn't a mean person, but fuck. That was some bullshit right there. He hadn't known Jordan's age when he had given Jordan his number. Then he had backed off and toned things down when he realized. Rhett slammed his car door and tried calming himself. It wasn't like him to storm off like that. His hands shook as he started his car.

The door to the coffee shop opened, catching his attention. He watched as Corey headed for his SUV. The way Corey moved had Rhett's temper slipping away. Rhett was good at reading people. Corey watched the ground when he walked, and he looked defeated as hell. Rhett blew out a sigh. Corey was the outcast. He also had a bluntness that showed an inability to read social cues. Rhett wondered if Corey was autistic or something similar. He felt like shit once he realized that was probably the case. More likely than not, Corey hadn't meant to insult him at all. His claim had likely been driven by statistics. Rhett scrubbed his forehead. Sometimes, he wished he wasn't such an empathetic person. He was too good at putting himself in other people's shoes. Even though he didn't know if any of his theories were true, it was too late. He had already created excuses for Corey in his head and now he felt guilty.

Rhett opened his car door. He would apologize. Corey backed from his spot and left before Rhett got the chance. Rhett closed his door again. It was for the best. He had known all along Corey was too good for him. It was time for Rhett to get back to what he knew. He needed to upload a new video anyhow. Then maybe he would hit Leather Bait tonight and take home one of his usual buddies. No need to dwell on what he couldn't have. No need at all. How depressing.

Corey lived in the odd position of having one foot in a life of crime and the other in the upmost respectability. He lived in a gated community, one where his closest neighbors couldn't hear anyone scream. The ocean was within a short golf cart drive. A members-only golf course was close enough he found golf balls in his pool all the time. To anyone who didn't know him, Corey was exactly what he seemed. He was a highly sought-after physician with a client list that was any doctor's wet dream. Corey was intelligent. Always had been. That wasn't a matter of conceit. It was a simple fact.

But Corey hadn't been handed this life of privilege on a silver platter. He had literally bled for it, paying for his place in life with screams, pain, and tears. Maybe he was unfeeling now. That didn't mean he didn't want to feel. It also didn't mean he couldn't recognize when he sabotaged his happiness. The problem was, making friends and building relationships meant exposing himself. Not just his place in life, but his heart and past. How could someone bubbly and confident like Rhett ever understand someone like him? Corey didn't want to be pitied. He wanted to be who he was now without having to look back. Corey didn't know enough about relationships to know if he would be allowed to exist without his past if he shared his life with someone else.

Corey scoffed as he lifted a beer bottle to his lips. He doubted someone like Rhett planned to settle down with anyone anyhow. Rhett might have come home with Corey for one night and not looked back. Corey paused with the bottle touching his bottom lip and stared out the glass back door at his pool. Was one night something he could do? He didn't know. Corey didn't date, much less have sex. Honestly, until Rhett burrowed his way into Corey's brain, Corey had thought of himself as asexual or at least demisexual. No one really appealed to him. Rhett did. Maybe he really was just repressed as hell.

With a shaky breath, Corey set his beer on the coffee table and moved to the couch. He sat and opened his phone. Corey didn't watch porn. As someone who had been exploited as a child, the idea of sex on camera was extremely distasteful to him. He opened Rhett's site while telling himself he only wanted to see Rhett's face. Corey hated himself for the way he had driven Rhett away. Likely, Rhett would never speak to him again. Corey just wanted to see him. As soon as the site loaded, Corey typed in his membership details, and a red flashing "live" icon caught his attention.

Rhett was live. Corey couldn't stop himself from clicking.

His breath caught at the images on the screen. The sounds Rhett made stirred something in Corey's gut. He watched Rhett fuck a rubber ass. There was a flashing butt plug blinking between his cheeks. Corey's skin heated. He tried to be analytical about the scene. His body didn't care what his mind wanted. Corey's cock stirred. Rhett flipped onto his back and toyed with the plug while his dick sawed in and out of the toy in his other hand. His body was perfect. The blinking light disappeared inside Rhett.

Rhett went still. "Um. Oh no." An uncomfortable laugh escaped him.

Corey leaned closer to the screen.

Rhett tried going in after the plug.

Corey shook his head. He already knew that wouldn't work alone.

Another uncomfortable laugh burst from Rhett. "Well, shit. That didn't go as planned."

Corey opened his messages and texted Rhett.

Corey: *Get dressed right now and come to my home clinic. 1140 Westbury Hills. The gate code is 1239. I can help.*

With the text sent, Corey moved the minimized video back to full screen. To his surprise, while still live, Rhett checked his phone.

"Thank fuck. Sorry to cut this short, but considering certain... things. I should get help. I'll make it up to everyone by uploading two videos next time."

Corey closed the feed and went to prep a room. If traffic was good, and Ransom's report on Rhett was up to date, Rhett could be here in under fifteen minutes from his apartment. He had the Xray machine warmed, lube out, and his smock on by the time the doorbell rang. Corey rushed to answer. He told himself he hurried because this was an emergency. But Corey knew he couldn't wait to see Rhett again, no matter the circumstances.

Rhett stood on the stoop in nothing but workout shorts, looking absolutely mortified. "This has never happened to me before."

As much as Corey wanted to smile, he didn't want Rhett to get the wrong impression. He was happy to see Rhett. Not laughing at him. It didn't matter how it happened. "I've got you. Come on. This is way more common than you think."

Rhett stepped inside. He looked ready to cry. Corey's heart twisted. If anyone understood sexual humiliation, it was Corey.

"Seriously. You don't need to be embarrassed with me. I'll take care of you." He took Rhett's hand and headed down the hall to his exam rooms.

"Why are you being nice to me now? I thought you didn't like me."

The motion sensor lights flared to life as they stepped inside the room. "Strip. Why would you think I don't like you?"

Rhett peeled off his shorts. "You all but called me a pedo earlier."

"Get on the table. I want to take an Xray to see where this toy has gone before I try to go in after it." He waited until Rhett did as told before addressing Rhett's claim. "I'm sorry I made you feel that way. Sometimes, when I think I'm just making conversation, everyone else thinks I'm being insulting." He set up the Xray machine and image cassette. "Don't move." Corey darted inside the protective room and took an image before moving to his computer. He returned to Rhett's side. "You're in luck, depending on how you look at things. It's not deep."

"Why is that dependent on how I look at things?"

Corey flashed him a wry smile. "It doesn't require anesthesia for me to go in after it."

Rhett stared at the ceiling. "Do it."

The resignation in Rhett's voice warmed something in Corey's chest. Maybe it was strange, but Rhett seemed more human in that moment than he had before. Corey fell back on his professionalism, hoping to make Rhett comfortable.

"Stand up and lean over the table. With any luck, I can do this quickly."

Rhett jumped from the table and did as directed.

Corey tried not to notice how perfect Rhett's huge body was in every way. He pulled on a pair of surgical gloves and lubed his hand. Corey set his non-lubed hand on the small of Rhett's back. "Relax and widen your stance."

"Is it awful that I know it's you behind me, so I'm having a hard time not making this sexual?" Rhett's voice came out, sounding muffled.

Corey fingered Rhett's ass. "Just try to think of this as a prostate exam."

Rhett chuckled. "But it's still you."

Corey smiled as he stretched Rhett and slowly slid deeper. Rhett was clenched and fighting him. He felt every time Rhett flinched from the pain. The harder Rhett fought, the deeper the plug went.

"Okay. You're fighting me. I'd like to try something else."

"Anything you say, doc."

Corey took a step back. "Back on the table."

Rhett climbed on the table and settled on his back again. His cock stood proudly. He flashed Corey a wicked smile. "Sorry. I told you, I know it's you."

Fuck. Corey was thankful for his smock because he wanted Rhett too. "As you said, it's me and we're friends. So I want to try something unusual."

Rhett nodded. Despite his aroused state, he still looked ready to cry. "Okay. Anything."

Corey nodded and moved the Xray machine out of the way. "Pull your knees up." While Rhett did what Corey told him to do, Corey climbed onto the table between Rhett's thighs. Rhett's gaze zeroed in on Corey and didn't budge. He looked turned on as hell. Corey wondered if he even breathed. "Have you ever bottomed for anyone?"

A flush rose on Rhett's cheeks. His cock jumped. "Yeah, but I prefer to top."

Corey figured as much. "Good. I want you to pretend you're ready to bottom for me."

Rhett's lips parted. He looked more aroused than any man had a right to be. Corey couldn't look away from his face. "Okay."

Corey scooted closer, positioning himself the way he would if he intended to fuck Rhett. He held Rhett's stare. "Relax. Open for me. Pretend it's my cock. Not my fingers." Corey slipped two fingers inside Rhett. He felt Rhett relax and tried for three and then four. "Don't you dare come yet. I'm just getting started."

"You're making it hard for me to see this as only pretending."

Corey smiled. He went in whole hand.

Rhett gasped. "I have questions." It was obvious Rhett tried distracting himself. "You said we were friends. So why are you always mean to me? I really like you. All I want is for you to like me too."

Corey was hard as a rock, and he wanted this to be more than medical care. It felt sexual to him as well. He knew the arousal had to show on his face too. Corey spoke without thinking while his mind turned to mush. "I do like you and I'm sorry if you think I'm mean. In my position, I have to stay calm and hard while still showing how much I care." He found the plug. Corey ensured he had a firm grip before slowly backing his way out. "I actually like you a lot. You have me ridiculously turned on right now, and that goes against all of my ethics. But it's you."

Rhett panted as if trapped somewhere between pleasure and pain. "If I come, I'm sorry. You're doing some wild shit to my mind and body right now."

The idea of making Rhett blow fucked with Corey's head. He wanted that. "I've got the plug. When it's out, I'm throwing it away. You're not risking this happening twice."

Rhett nodded. "Understood."

Corey quickly pulled his hand away, extracting the toy as he went.

Rhett cried out.

He didn't come, so Corey didn't think the sound had been one of pleasure. "Sorry. I'll give you something for the pain."

Rhett's crazed stare met Corey's gaze. "I don't want anything for the pain. I want you."

Corey held his breath. While holding Rhett's stare, Corey's fingers found Rhett's asshole again. Rhett gasped. Corey knew he would be sore. This time, he only slipped two fingers inside. He found Rhett's prostate and rubbed. Rhett's chest heaved like he ran a marathon. His eyes looked wild—like he might snap at any second. Fascinated, Corey kept massaging while he gripped Rhett's erection with his free hand.

"You'll be sore tomorrow."

Rhett gripped the edge of the table and whimpered.

Corey stroked faster. "I think you're sexy as hell. You're also incredibly sweet. I know I'm not easy to get to know, but I want to know you."

"Yes. Fuck. Please? I like you a lot. Like, a lot, a lot. Would you like to meet my mom?" His back bowed. "Goddamn. I think I'd give you my last name at this point. I take back what I said about you being mean. You're very, very nice."

A bright smile exploded across Corey's face. Rhett went still and held Corey's stare. "Wow. You really are so beautiful."

At the compliment, Corey leaned in and licked Rhett's dick from root to tip before swallowing him. Rhett's entire body jerked. Cum filled Corey's mouth. Corey immediately spit it out. It had been instinctual. The taste of cum triggered him. He closed his eyes and focused on breathing.

"So, you subscribe to my channel, huh?"

Like that, all the ugliness vanished. A snort escaped Corey. He still couldn't look at Rhett. "Yeah. Since we met."

Rhett made a humming sound. It was soothing for reasons Corey couldn't explain. "You want to be my boyfriend?"

Corey's smile somehow got brighter. Happy tears clogged his throat. He kissed Rhett's stomach so Rhett wouldn't see the myriad of emotions choking him. "I'd like that."

Rhett stroked his hair. "Good. Me too."

Corey let the moment soothe him. He had survived a new step toward recovery. It felt amazing. He also discovered something about Rhett he couldn't unlearn. Rhett was exactly who he seemed to be. How had he lived this long?

CHAPTER FOUR

RHETT WAS THIRTY-FOUR YEARS old, and he still got excited when the school bell rang, setting him free for the day. He didn't always get to leave at the same time as the students, but that bell still made him smile. Today, he didn't wait that long. Since the last period of the day was technically his planning period and Rhett didn't have anything to do, he cut out early. While he hadn't spoken with Corey yet, Rhett hoped he could convince Corey to spend the night with him. Corey hadn't let him return any favors last night. He had gently cleaned Rhett's body and then made him dinner. Honestly, he was a bit insecure about the entire ordeal. Not only had Corey not let Rhett touch him in return, but they also hadn't even kissed. It was strange. He worried he had misread things. Maybe Corey didn't want to date him after all.

Rhett headed to his SUV with his mind churning over the problem. He would call Corey when he got on the road. Everything would be okay. Rhett would make Corey happy. He would see.

"Rhett."

Rhett slowed at the sound of his name. He turned. His heart dropped at the sight of Marshall heading his way. His long stride ate up the distance between them while dark curls danced in the breeze.

A too-white smile lit Marshall's face. His amber eyes crinkled in the corners. "Hey. Don't worry, I'm not stalking you. I was parked over there waiting to pick up Terry." He motioned to a nearby spot. "How are you? Did you end up at the ER last night?"

Rhett blinked. "What?"

Marshall's smile faltered. "You must not have gotten my email. I subscribe to your channel." Marshall dropped his voice and leaned closer. "I'm the one who sent you eight hundred dollars to fuck a watermelon. How was that, by the way?"

Rhett didn't have a lot of shame, but he was at his job, and everything about this situation was horrific. He couldn't find his voice.

Marshall made a dismissive gesture. "Don't worry. I won't say anything. I imagine you'd probably lose your job if anyone knew."

Rhett cleared his throat. He couldn't decide if Marshall's words were a veiled threat. "Yeah. Most likely."

"Really," Marshall said, holding up his hands as if in surrender. "I won't tell anyone. It was just a shock to me when I realized where I had seen you before. I never suspected we lived in the same town. You do a great job of keeping your personal information a secret. Trust me. I looked."

Honest to God, Rhett didn't know how to respond. There were people in his real life who knew about his channel, but they all belonged to his fetish club and everything that happened there was like fight club. Rhett never expected a parent to find his content. "Did you need something?"

Marshall went from staring intently at Rhett to shaking his head and smiling. "Sorry. No. I mean, yeah. Would you like to have dinner with me one night? Like a date."

Now they were in territory Rhett could handle. He donned his most charming smile. "If I was a single man, I would definitely say yes, but I'm not." He definitely would not say yes because this bordered on creepy, but Marshall didn't know that.

Marshall's smile faltered a hair. Disappointment filled his amber eyes. "Oh. Okay. They're lucky to have you. But I'm sure he... she knows that already..." Marshall looked at him questioningly.

"He. His name is Corey, and I hope so," Rhett added with a laugh.

Marshall took a step back. He was two inches taller than Rhett, and Rhett was a tall guy, so he appreciated the distance. "If you ever feel unappreciated, you should look me up. I own Marshall's Pool Company, so I'm easy to find."

Rhett held on to his smile. "I'll keep that in mind. It was great seeing you again."

Marshall winked and turned away.

Rhett climbed inside his Bronco with his heart racing. Marshall claimed he wouldn't say anything, but rejected men were capable of anything. Rhett had learned that lesson many times in his life. The moment he started the vehicle and got the air flowing, he called Corey. He needed Corey's calm voice to steady him.

"Dr. A. speaking."

"Hello, gorgeous. Do you have plans tonight?"

"I'm in California."

Rhett rubbed his forehead. "Oh. Okay."

Silence dragged on between them while Rhett silently panicked over his future.

Corey spoke and pulled him away from the edge. "Tell me what's wrong. It's not like you to be quiet."

A genuine smile snapped to Rhett's lips. His mood immediately lifted. "Hey. I can be quiet. It's just rare for it to happen. You're right this time, though. I had a bad day." Or a bad five minutes that ruined his whole day, but that was beside the point. "I just hoped I could see you tonight. Do you know, other than that quick kiss I stole on our first date, you haven't even kissed me?"

"That day didn't count as a date. It was a kidnapping. Why was your day bad?"

Rhett put his car in reverse. Marshall was completely forgotten. "Oh, I see how it is now. You just change the subject and never, ever kiss me. That's unacceptable. I have great lips. You should taste them."

"Why are you avoiding my question?"

Rhett couldn't explain why he liked this monotone single-mindedness Corey possessed, but it always made him smile so big, his face hurt. "It's just boring work stuff. Nothing big. I hate I can't see you right now."

"You can. It's called FaceTime."

"I'm driving."

"I was wrong. FaceTime doesn't exist. You should definitely only focus on your task."

Rhett laughed at Corey's deadpan reversal. "You don't have to worry. I never do anything crazy while driving. Sometimes, I'm given Driver's Ed duties, so I'm hyperaware of setting an example."

"You're just a genuinely good person, aren't you?"

Rhett's forehead furrowed at Corey's tone. "You say that like you aren't."

Corey didn't even miss a beat. "I'm not."

"Well, I happen to think you're amazing."

Corey snorted. "Have you ever met anyone you don't like? I'm not sure you're the best judge of character."

"Was that a snort?" Rhett asked, avoiding the question because he did like almost everyone he met. "I made you snort. Adorable."

A low murmur came from the background. "Put him in room two. I'll be there in a moment," Corey said to who-ever interrupted them. "I'm sorry."

"Hey, you're a superhero. You have to go. I get it," Rhett said before Corey felt guilty over having a job. "I miss you, though."

"You haven't known me long enough to miss me."

Rhett rolled his eyes. "Does that mean you don't miss me?"

Corey didn't respond right away. When he did, he sounded mildly surprised. "Actually, I do."

Everything was right in the world at that moment. Corey missed him. "See me when you get back in town."

"Of course. I'll text you as soon as I'm home."

Rhett bit his bottom lip for a moment. His smile was out of control. "Okay." Even he heard the happiness in that one word.

"See you later, beautiful."

Rhett disconnected the call and squealed in excitement. Corey had called him beautiful. It was the first time in his life Rhett felt like someone meant it as a genuine compliment. Corey wasn't the type to flatter people. Rhett took a breath. He couldn't wait to see Corey again. He might burst with excitement before then. Life had never looked so promising.

Exhaustion weighed heavily on Corey, making him wonder if he had lost his mind. Maybe meeting Rhett had really messed with his head. As far as Rhett knew, Corey was still in California. Rhett very well might have called someone else to lift his mood. Corey might have flown home the second he could just to find out Rhett wasn't alone. In fact, he felt certain that was exactly what would happen as he parked outside Rhett's apartment.

There was a light on inside. Otherwise, Corey might have talked himself into going home. He still couldn't believe he had come here like an addict looking for his next hit. As Corey knocked on the front door, he wondered if he wanted Rhett to answer. The porch light flared to life. A half second passed before the door opened. Rhett's hair was a mess, but his idiotic smile was like a hit of adrenaline.

"Hey. I thought you were in California."

Corey nodded. "I was, but you said you had a bad day, so I came home."

Rhett pulled a face and touched his chest, as if Corey's words moved him. "That's so sweet. I don't even know what to say." He startled. "Oh, yeah. Come in. Sorry. I didn't mean to leave you standing outside."

Corey stepped inside and fought the urge to shake his head. Rhett made him question his sanity. He was a bit goofy, and Corey just really liked him and felt good in his company. The entire situation was as ridiculous as things got for him.

"Have a seat. Do you want anything to drink? I was just watching TV."

Corey picked a spot on the cushy-looking leather couch and sat. "I'm good."

Rhett filled the spot beside him, sitting as close as possible. "You know, you still haven't told me what the A stands for."

"Abayantsev. It's Russian."

Rhett chuckled. "So you do have a name. Why do you call yourself Dr. A?"

Corey couldn't help but smile. Everything about Rhett was contagious. "Because most people can't pronounce Abayantsev, and there's a huge backlash against Russians at the moment. I wasn't raised there and know next to nothing about the place or the people who so—" Corey cleared his throat. "My biological parents."

"Did you start to say the people who sold you?"

Corey flashed a tight smile. "It happens more than you think."

Rhett traced the shell of Corey's ear with his fingertip. His gaze followed the motion, leaving Corey free to look at him without fear of being watched. "It's all the details like that I want to know about you. You're unique."

In spite of himself, Corey smiled. "Unique isn't usually a good thing. People tend to mean 'weird' when they call me that."

Rhett's gaze moved his way, catching him staring. "I don't think you're weird. Is it okay if I kiss you now?"

Since that was the real reason Corey was there, he couldn't say no. He gave Rhett a jerky nod. He wasn't the least bit confident at that moment. "Yes."

Rhett didn't give him time to think, which was probably a good thing. Rhett's mouth covered his, and Corey's lips automatically parted. Corey realized it was almost laughable that he had never considered himself a sexual person. It seemed he had simply been waiting for Rhett. Somehow, Corey found himself straddling Rhett's lap, and he didn't recall moving. Rhett's kiss was that mesmerizing.

Corey leaned away. "Don't ask questions, okay?" He took off his shirt and came back for more.

Rhett didn't fail him. He didn't make a single inquiry about the massive scarring on Corey's torso. Of course, he might not have noticed. Corey did his best to keep Rhett distracted. Their tongues played while Corey worked on divesting Rhett of his shirt. Rhett practically ripped the piece of clothing from his back so he could return to kissing Corey. Corey had never felt so powerful. Rhett seemed desperate for him. Then their bare torsos met, and Corey reached a new level of arousal. He thought he might burst into flames. As Corey dug his short nails into Rhett's skin, trying to get closer, the world tilted. Corey found himself beneath Rhett on the couch. He didn't try to steal Corey's pants. It was like he made love to Corey in his clothes.

Rhett moved restlessly against him. While their tongues battled, Rhett's hips rocked. Corey was torn between wanting to tear off Rhett's pants and savoring the friction between them. Above every emotion swirling inside him, Corey felt safe. He knew Rhett wouldn't attack. The entire encounter was two-sided. They were equally engrossed and mutually moving toward the goal of release. Honestly, it was even more than that. It was as if they were mentally consumed by each other. Corey didn't sleep with anyone. It was possible Rhett only toyed with him. Rhett definitely possessed the tools to play him, but Corey knew in his heart that wasn't true. They wanted something more than sex from each other. They were almost too desperate for the encounter to only be about pleasure. Corey wondered if Rhett felt like something was missing in his soul too. Rhett felt like Corey's missing piece.

"You're about to make me come in my jeans."

"Good." Corey wanted that to happen.

Rhett chuckled against his lips. "I have clothes to change into and you don't."

Fuck. That was true.

"And there's no way in hell I'm coming alone again. I want to watch you fly."

A hint of panic hit Corey. He didn't want to take off his pants. Not yet.

Rhett touched his forehead to Corey's and held his stare. With his weight balanced on one hand, Rhett reached between them and easily unbuttoned Corey's jeans. "I just want to touch you. Don't you want to touch me?"

Corey took a breath. It sounded ragged as hell. He unbuttoned Rhett's jeans. A pant escaped Rhett as Corey unzipped his jeans. Rhett mimicked Corey, unzipping Corey's jeans. Corey realized Rhett followed him, going only as far as Corey did. He set Rhett's cock free and rubbed. Rhett did the same for Corey. A loud pant burst from Corey. Rhett gently pushed Corey's hand away and ground his erection against Corey's. Corey reclaimed Rhett's mouth.

This time, they kissed slow. They savored each other while Rhett used the friction between them to pleasure them. Corey had never made love like this.

Hell, he had never made love. He'd been fucked. Used. This was different. It was soul stealing. Pleasure and pressure built, driving him insane. His skin felt too tight. He wanted more. Corey needed something just out of reach. Then Rhett's thrusts quickened. His breathing turned more ragged by the second. Corey whimpered, clawing his way closer to madness. Unexpectedly, a cry tore from his throat as the irritating pressure exploded into blinding pleasure. Sounds he couldn't control left him as Rhett rocked every spasm from him. Rhett's cries mixed with his. The space between them was a hot mess of cum. With their jeans half down their hips, Corey hoped their clothes were mostly spared, but he wasn't sure he cared any longer. He was more worried about how he would never be the same after this. Rhett had ruined him.

Even after cleaning them and settling back in for all the snuggles, Rhett couldn't stop kissing Corey. He was too smitten. Rhett couldn't think of another word to describe the giddiness, hunger, and hope that roiled inside him. Corey made him feel something he hadn't in a long time. But Rhett also recognized there was a lot he didn't know, and he hadn't completely pierced Corey's armor yet.

Rhett kissed the corner of Corey's mouth. "Mhmm. I'm sorry. I can't stop."

A sexy chuckle rumbled from Corey. "Good."

Without thinking, Rhett's fingers traced the ragged ridges of a deep scar on

Corey's stomach. "How can you expect me not to have questions?"

"You can have questions."

Rhett fought a laugh at Corey's choice of wording. He hadn't granted Rhett permission to ask anything. Only given him permission to be curious. "Why are you so mysterious? You make me wonder if I'm getting played and if tomorrow you'll never call again."

"I don't play games."

Rhett knew that. He just didn't know how to explain the insecurity that went along with Corey's refusal to let him in. "Do you not think of me as your real boyfriend?" Rhett asked the question slowly, thinking over each word. He immediately felt stupid and raced to explain. "I mean, we haven't really set boundaries yet and I don't know if I'm smart enough to really keep up with you or anything. I just... ugh. Never mind. I just hate the idea of you being with anyone else, but I also realize you might have not meant for us to be exclusive. Plus, you're not really letting me in or anything. I'm trying to get to know you, but you act like you don't want that. Never mind," Rhett said again, vowing this time he would be quiet.

Corey kissed the corner of his mouth.

Rhett took a steadying breath.

Corey stroked his arm, soothing him. "I was stabbed forty-seven times when I was eleven, and yes. We're exclusive if that's what you want. I mean, I don't date, so that was never a fear on my side of things anyhow."

Rhett's heart twisted in his chest. "Forty-seven times? You were a kid. Who would do that to a kid?"

A sweet smile touched Corey's lips. "You're a good person. Most people aren't."

"Will you tell me why someday?" He didn't need to know now. Rhett just needed to know the topic wasn't closed.

"One day."

Rhett nodded. "Okay." His hand smoothed across Corey's stomach like it had a mind of its own. "Will you stay the night with me?"

Corey nodded. His gaze never wavered from holding Rhett's stare. Rhett felt himself falling into Corey's blue eyes. There was something incredibly innocent about Corey. Rhett couldn't put his finger on why, but Corey's mannerisms appealed to Rhett in an unexpected way. For all his adult life, Rhett had surrounded himself with men who would do anything with no strings attached.

Then Corey had come along, and suddenly, Rhett wanted all the ties he could manage so Corey wouldn't get away. Life was funny sometimes. As he kissed Corey again, Rhett wondered if he had finally matured. He blew a raspberry on Corey's bottom lip and laughed until he thought he would cry at Corey's shocked expression. It had been a test. He wasn't an adult yet. Still, he wanted this.

CHAPTER FIVE

"WHAT DO YOU DO for someone you care about when they're having a bad day?"

Bear didn't respond to Corey's question right away, which was fair. They had been silently working side by side for nearly an hour before Corey ambushed him with the question. Plus, Corey never asked for advice. He imagined Bear was shocked. For a moment, the bald, tattooed, and muscle-bound mercenary stared into space as if Corey's question confused him. Then a slow, wicked smile touched his lips. He shook his head.

"I'm probably not the right person to ask. My husband is kinky as fuck. What I'd do for him probably doesn't count in your situation, and there's no one else who would look for me if they needed to feel better."

Corey was honestly a little surprised to learn that about Bear's husband. Creed seemed incredibly straitlaced. "Does Creed know what you do? I mean, for real?"

"Of course," Bear said without missing a beat. "You can't have a successful marriage built on lies."

That gave Corey hope. Bear was an extermination specialist. If he could tell his husband about his work, then Corey, being the person who handled the care of the team and of the rescued children, might be accepted too.

"Who's this mystery person anyhow? I've never heard you talk about anyone before."

"His name is Rhett Porter."

Bear's eyebrows rose. "*The* Rhett Porter? The porn guy from Leather Bait, who has everyone panting after him?"

Corey shrugged, feeling uncomfortable. "I've never been to Leather Bait, so I don't know anything about that, but yeah. He has a porn channel."

A low whistle rent the air. Bear looked flabbergasted. "I never talked to him or anything, but I used to see him around all the time back when I lived in town and went to the club. If you'd like, I can ask Creed what you could do to brighten his day and catch his eye. Creed knows all the members' kinks."

"He's already my boyfriend. I'm just not good at reading social cues, so I don't know how to make people happy when they're down."

Bear looked like Corey could knock him over with a feather. "You're dating pretty but dumb Porter?"

Corey's temper spiked. "He's not dumb. He's a schoolteacher."

A line appeared between Bear's eyebrows. "Really?" Bear's face cleared. He shrugged. "Like I said, we've never spoken. That was just me repeating what people say about him at Leather Bait. That's cool, though. He seems really bubbly. That's exactly what you need." Bear looked thoughtful for a moment. They were cleaning exam rooms after having spent the day treating a new batch of incoming rescued children. They needed the distraction of Corey's newfound love life. Days like today were always soul crushing. Finally, a huge smile lit Bear's face. "You should buy him a brightly decorated cake. He looks like the life-of-the-party type. Go to a bakery and get the most over-the-top neon-colored cake you can find and surprise him. Everyone likes having a regular Thursday unexpectedly turned into their birthday. Rhett looks like the kind of guy who would extra appreciate something like that."

That was a good idea, and it was one he wouldn't have thought of on his own. "Thank you. That was exactly the type of advice I was looking for, and I might try that." Corey decided to change the subject. He hated talking about himself. "How is Creed enjoying living in Washington?"

The way Bear smiled at the mention of his husband sent an unwanted spike of jealousy through Corey. He didn't know if he would ever be as adjusted. "Good. He'd planned to join the police force there after the move, but after a few weeks at home, we both realized how much we love the flexibility of him being a househusband. So he's not going back to work. You know how it is. I travel all the time and we'd never get to see each other if we had to work around his schedule too."

Corey nodded. He had already made one rushed trip home just to see Rhett. It would likely be that way a lot if he hoped to see Rhett regularly. "That's understandable."

With the exam room cleaned, Bear jumped onto the table and sat. He focused on Corey, forcing Corey to find some place else to look. "So how did you meet Rhett?"

Corey removed his personal items from his smock so he could send the soiled jacket with the cleaning crew. "Through a friend. The Butcher's new husband, Jordan. I don't know if you've met him yet."

"Not yet. I've been busy."

"He's nice." Corey flashed Bear a smile. "Really sweet."

Bear nodded, looking strangely serious. "That's good to hear. Timofey deserves a soft place to land. So do you, by the way. I'm glad to know you're dating someone who'll drag you along for the ride."

Corey smiled at the image Bear painted. "I suppose that's exactly what dating Rhett is like."

"Is it okay if I ask you an uncomfortable question?"

The vulnerability in Bear's voice had Corey meeting his stare. "Yes."

Bear shifted nervously, making Corey's curiosity spike. For a moment, Bear kept moving his hands from his sides to his lap and then back again, before he finally spoke. "It's been over twenty years since you were in the same place as these boys. Do you think..." Bear went back to shifting uncomfortably before trying again. "Do you think we're actually saving anyone?"

Corey didn't hesitate. "Yes. I know we are. Every day they wake up alive and free is a day they won."

A sweet smile touched Bear's lips. "Good. That's good." He slapped his knees. "Well, I guess I should head to the in-laws' place before Creed's mom convinces him to leave me."

An unexpected laugh burst from Corey. "Does she not like you?"

Bear shrugged. "I think she likes me just fine, but I moved her baby to the other side of the country."

"So convince his parents to move too. It can't be that hard."

Bear hesitated, as if that thought hadn't occurred to him before now. "Maybe I'll do that."

Corey waved Bear away with a smile. He felt good about himself today. It wasn't often anyone spoke to him about anything other than work. They definitely never asked him for advice. He didn't feel so much like an outsider today. Maybe he would get that cake when he finished working. It seemed like a good day to celebrate.

With a dozen red roses and a bottle of wine in hand, Rhett headed for Corey's front door. He hadn't called ahead. Likely, he should have, but he wanted to surprise Corey. Rhett doubted anyone ever did anything nice for him. He wanted to be the one who gave Corey all the good memories. Before he had time to ring the doorbell, the door opened, and a familiar figure stepped out. Rhett only knew the guy's name because he had married a friend of Rhett's from Leather Bait. Still, it was a bit off-putting to suddenly run into Bear at Corey's.

A bright smile exploded across Bear's face when they nearly collided. "Hey. It's Rhett, right?"

Rhett nodded. "Bear, right?"

Bear nodded as he eyed the gifts Rhett had brought for Corey. "I heard you were dating Dr. A. That's awesome. He needs someone to keep him on his toes."

Rhett's usual bright smile snapped into place. "That's me. I can do that."

A chuckle rumbled from Bear, as if Rhett amused him. "He's in the exam room." Bear stepped aside to let Rhett in as he made the claim.

Rhett stepped inside. "I thought Creed and you moved to Washington or something like that. Are you a patient of Corey's?"

Bear nodded. "Yep. Dr. A. is the best. Creed and I are in town, visiting family. I thought I'd get my yearly checkup while I was here."

Rhett pulled a face. "Yikes. Don't remind me. I need to do that too, but I'm always putting it off."

"Well, you're dating a doctor, so..."

Rhett brightened. "Hey, you're right. I never have to go to the doctor again."

Bear laughed. "It was good seeing you."

"You too. Tell Creed I said hi."

"Will do," Bear said as he pulled the door closed behind him. Rhett immediately focused on finding his man. He headed down the hallway, following the path he had taken the last time he had been there. When Rhett stepped inside the exam room, he found Corey on a rolling stool with his head resting on his crossed arms on the exam table. Rhett's heart dropped at the sight. He looked so tired.

"Are you okay, baby?"

Corey visibly startled and turned toward the door. "Hey. I didn't hear the doorbell."

Rhett moved deeper into the room. "Bear let me in on his way out. Did I come at a bad time?"

"No such thing. I'm happy to see you."

It felt good to hear that. Corey wasn't one to say how he felt. Rhett shook the flowers and wine in Corey's direction. "I stopped by the store and grabbed these as a pick-me-up, and I thought you might like to share them with me."

Corey looked confused.

Rhett laughed. "I'm joking. They're for you."

A sweet smile touched Corey's lips as Rhett passed him the flowers. "Thank you. I'll admit I've always thought of flowers as a ridiculous gift since they die, but I'm strangely moved."

Rhett snorted. "I think I might've been disappointed by any other reaction," Rhett said, sounding as if the words had been more for himself than Corey. He chose one of the chairs lining the wall and sat. "You do know that's kind of the point of buying someone flowers, don't you? It's a waste of money. Nothing says I like you so much I don't care that I'm dropping fifty dollars on flowers that'll be dead in three days."

Corey blinked at the roses. "You paid fifty dollars for these?"

The horror in Corey's voice had Rhett's smile growing. "I would've paid a hundred to see that reaction. You're all I thought about today."

At Rhett's confession, Corey met his stare. He looked how Rhett felt: intoxicated. Rhett realized something massive. They wanted this equally. Neither of them was playing or passing time. This was real.

Rhett couldn't stop baring his heart. "You're the best thing that's happened to me in a long time."

Corey looked taken aback by the confession. He cleared his throat. "I'm glad I didn't kill you when you dragged me from the bakery against my will."

A laugh burst from Rhett. Corey's dry sense of humor was just one of a million irresistible things about him. "You're funny."

Corey clutched the flowers to his chest. "Would you like to stay the night?"

Rhett couldn't think of a single thing he wanted to do more. Even a SWAT team couldn't drag him away. Corey had shown him affection, and now he was stuck with Rhett. That was the way it worked. There was no going back.

CHAPTER SIX

COREY COOKED. RHETT WANTED to, since Corey was obviously exhausted, but he wouldn't let Rhett do anything. He was an amazing chef. With each new detail, Rhett wondered if they should bother dating. Rhett thought he might need to skip to marrying Corey before he got away. It seemed wrong no one had scooped him up yet. Rhett wanted the job.

With the wine consumed, Rhett lured Corey into the living room for cuddles. "Come on, beautiful. I want snuggles. Drop everything and let me hold you.

I promise I'll clean the kitchen in the morning."

Corey looked exactly like a man fighting an eye roll. "You don't have to bribe me. I enjoy cuddling with you. Am I doing something to make you think I don't?" Corey didn't sound upset. He sounded more curious than anything—like he tried searching for the answer online.

Rhett pulled Corey onto his lap on the couch. "Nope." He kissed Corey's neck. "You're just difficult to read. That's okay, though. I find it endearing."

Even though Corey buried his fingers in Rhett's hair and held on while Rhett enjoyed his neck, when he spoke, his voice still sounded unaffected. "I don't know why you'd think I'm hard to read. If you have a question, I'll answer it. I'm not a coy person."

Rhett chuckled against Corey's skin. "You're overthinking things."

A hitched breath escaped Corey as Rhett licked a path to Corey's shoulder. "Sorry. I don't have a flirtatious setting, or maybe it's just broken."

Rhett had lost interest in the conversation. The way Corey responded in his arms didn't require words. "Everyone has a flirtatious setting. Have you tried unplugging it and plugging it back in?"

"Damn. Don't stop. That feels good."

Rhett smiled against Corey's throat. "I don't think you need to worry about—"

A loud alarm sounded, sending Corey scrambling from Rhett's lap. For a moment, Rhett sat stunned as Corey raced from the room. The clanging came from the distance. After a second, the ringing stopped, only to be replaced by shouting voices. Rhett shot to his feet and followed the sound. It didn't sound like people were yelling in anger. The voices were more panicked or hurried. Still, Rhett didn't dally. If Corey was in the midst of confronting an intruder or something, Rhett needed to help.

He slid around the corner and into a living nightmare. A small child, probably no more than five, was on a gurney. Blood covered so much of him that Rhett didn't recognize him as a person at first. A lanky man with dirty blond hair straddled the bloodied heap, doing chest compressions while Bear tried keeping pressure on several wounds at once. It looked like a losing battle.

Corey rapidly pulled on his surgical gear—like going into battle.

Bear sounded panicked. "I don't know how we missed him. Ender was helping the crew clean the scene when he found him. I thought he was dead."

Rhett pressed against the wall, trying to stay out of the way while his mind refused to work. His legs wouldn't budge. Horror kept him completely frozen in place.

"Goddamn it. You've got to fight, kid," Corey yelled while starting an IV. "Take over this." Corey motioned for Bear. "We have to get blood in him if we have any hope of saving him."

With blood-soaked clothes and arms, Bear jumped in to work on the IV while Corey grabbed a machine and pulled it close. "Clear the body, Dante. I'll have to shock him."

The lanky blond jumped from the table. He was every bit as wild-eyed as Rhett imagined he looked. Everyone stood clear while Corey shocked the tiny boy.

His fragile body left the gurney in a spasm, but no heartbeat showed on the screen.

"Bump it up, Bear."

Bear turned a knob, and Corey shocked him again. He got the same result. Silence filled the room. Blood poured onto the floor. A heartbeat passed. Corey's shoulders heaved.

"One more. We're not giving up."

He shocked the kid's heart again. A tiny beat appeared. It wasn't much, but it was life.

"There we go, kid. Fight. Just give me time."

The three men jumped in together and went to work. Corey was the only one wearing any protection from the blood, but none of them seemed to care about the mess. Rhett couldn't see what they were doing. He was a little grateful for that. Instead, he kept his gaze locked on the small face that was turned his way. It was oddly clean. The boy looked like he had been thrown through the windshield of a car... or someone had used him as a punching bag.

Rhett's feet moved. He couldn't stop. While he possessed zero medical training beyond CPR and how to use a defibrillator, he couldn't let a kid do this alone. Rhett snagged Corey's rolling stool and moved to the head of the gurney where he was out of the way and stroked the boy's hair. Rhett leaned close and whispered soothing words while Corey worked. He didn't look the other men's way. Rhett didn't care what anyone thought. This child was alone. He would never leave one of his students to suffer without a parent. This was no different. He couldn't let this kid go through this alone.

The longer the men worked, the stronger the boy's heartbeat became. Corey repaired wounds while Bear kept the blood bags coming, and the guy Rhett didn't know kept pressure on open wounds until Corey made it to those.

Hours passed, but Rhett didn't notice. He was too busy lending the boy his strength. More people came and went. Rhett never stopped focusing on the child enduring the worst nightmare Rhett had ever seen. Then his new friend was tightly bandaged. First, the lanky guy left and returned in clean scrubs. Bear followed. When Bear returned in clean scrubs, Corey left, but Rhett never moved. No one spoke. There was nothing to say.

Corey came back into the room, wearing black pajama pants and a white t-shirt.

Bear finally broke the silence. "Creed is on his way. We'll stay with the kid. You two get some sleep. If he crashes in the middle of the night, you'll need your rest."

Corey squeezed Rhett's shoulder, making him realize Bear had been talking to them. His hair was wet from the shower, making Rhett realize how deep his shock went. Reality felt far away. "Come on, baby. If he lives, he won't be awake for a long while."

Corey sounded like a different person. It might have been exhaustion, or possibly Rhett saw the real him for once. Either way, Rhett automatically obeyed. He stood and cast one last look at the tiny child. Rhett had so many questions, he didn't know where to start, but he knew one thing without a hint of doubt. Corey was special. He was a warrior. Corey had been put on this earth with a gift like nothing Rhett had ever witnessed before. He had snatched a kid's soul out of death's hands. Rhett had no words.

When they reached the bedroom. Corey's gaze moved over Rhett's body, as if checking him for blood. "You should take a shower. I keep plenty of fresh scrubs and pajamas in several sizes just for nights like tonight. I'll find you something to wear and toss your clothes in the wash."

He sounded so calm.

With a nod, Rhett headed for the bathroom that was inside the bedroom. The light was on, and steam still lingered in the air from where Corey had obviously taken a shower. He didn't bother closing the door. Rhett undressed on autopilot and stepped inside the shower. His mind shied away from everything he had witnessed. He wasn't a robot or a seasoned veteran. When Rhett's teeth chattered, he knew the shock had come for him. Luckily, it passed while he scrubbed his body. Still, his hands shook as he dried himself and pulled on the black pajama pants Corey had left for him. His clothes were gone. It was like Rhett's brain worked, but it didn't. He replayed everything that had happened and still the numbness wouldn't ease. Then he left the bathroom and found Corey sitting quietly in a chair near the bed. He looked every bit as wrecked as Rhett felt, and Rhett realized Corey wasn't unaffected in any way. He was just better at hiding it.

Rhett sat on the edge of the bed.

Corey didn't look at him. He visibly swallowed. "You can't tell anyone about what happened here tonight."

Rhett's confusion doubled. "What would I tell? I'm still not even sure what happened."

Corey nodded while staring at the corner. He looked on the verge of tears. "That's fair." Corey cleared his throat. "I don't know where to start other than the beginning." His gaze finally moved Rhett's way. Corey's eyes looked sad—like he was broken inside, and his calm was only an illusion. It was Rhett's first real look behind the mask Corey wore. Rhett couldn't look away. "First I need your word you won't repeat anything said here."

"You have it." There was no way Rhett would betray Corey. After the miracle he had witnessed tonight, he was convinced Corey was pure magic.

Corey gave him a jerky nod and cleared his throat again. "I was born into a poor family by parents who wanted me... until they didn't. They hadn't planned for me to be different. I wasn't a baby they could hold and rock, the way they expected. The opposite, in fact. I screamed whenever anyone touched me and melted down at loud sounds. They thought they could force me to be what they wanted, but their efforts only made me worse. Then they had a second child, and three years of my difficulty was enough. Their new baby was what they'd hoped to have the first time. So they sold me to what they thought was a wealthy family."

Rhett could barely blink as he watched Corey tell the story of his childhood with zero emotion.

"They thought they were giving me a better life with someone who possessed the means to get me the help I needed to learn healthy coping methods. Obviously, they made a lot of money on the exchange, but the only other option was an orphanage and they honestly believed they were giving me a better life. I have no malice toward them. Unfortunately, they were duped. I was immediately tossed onto a cargo ship with dozens of other children and brought here to America. When we arrived, we were auctioned to the highest bidder. Some children went to personal buyers. Others, like me, were sold to homes where we were prostituted to pedophiles."

Rhett covered his mouth, even though he didn't know why. He couldn't have made a sound if he tried. His throat no longer worked.

Corey went back to staring at the corner while he spoke. "As I said, I screamed whenever anyone touched me, but that didn't matter to this home. Some men liked that and would pay extra for the fight. One night, though, a customer got carried away and stabbed me. Then he didn't stop. Afterward, I was dumped in an alleyway. A homeless man found me and carried me to the ER. I grew up in the system and used my intelligence to my advantage, getting scholarships and graduating at the top of every school I attended."

Corey's gaze moved back Rhett's way, as if the worst of it was done and he could look at Rhett again. "During my internship at an L.A. County emergency room, I was approached by a man with an offer to work for a private entity. This man knew all about me. He knew literally everything. Every gap in my memory.

He had the answer. He told me there were hundreds of children arriving in the US almost daily, being sold into the same fate I suffered. The money he offered was enough no one could turn it down, but I think I would've said yes for free." Corey fell silent and Rhett filled in the blanks. He saved victims of sex trafficking. Rhett couldn't even imagine. The psychological damage Corey suffered on the daily had to be massive. While it was obvious from Corey's story that he was in some part autistic, Rhett realized now Corey's mannerisms were more likely about protecting his sanity. Rhett had never been prouder to know anyone.

"So you save kids for a living."

A bark of humorless laughter burst from Corey, even as a tear rolled down his cheek. "Probably not tonight."

Rhett couldn't tear his gaze away from that one tear. It ripped out his heart. Even as his throat tried swelling closed, he couldn't stop trying to be closer to Corey. "Who saves you?"

Corey took a ragged-sounding breath. His entire chest stuttered, as if it fought not to cave. "No one."

"Then I do." Rhett was on his feet in an instant. He crossed the room and lifted Corey from the chair. "I want the job." Rhett carried Corey to bed with determination filling his heart. Corey was amazing. Rhett planned to keep him and take care of him like no one else had before. Corey was his now. He would find out what it meant to have a real home. Rhett would save him.

Corey couldn't recall the last time his heart stayed locked in his throat like this. He wasn't scared to talk about his past. Corey might not enjoy doing so, but he could. He had been to enough therapy and helped enough victims that he knew he wasn't damaged or anything other such nonsense. Tonight had just been especially rough. This victim had been much younger than they usually were when they came to Corey. He had also been in much worse shape. Corey honestly didn't expect he would make it through the night. If he did, he would never be the same. He would need more help than Corey could give him.

Rhett had been fantastic. Corey didn't doubt for a second Rhett had been the real one keeping that kid alive. Now, Corey felt vulnerable and exposed in a way he hadn't in years. He didn't know how to move past it, but being in Rhett's arms was a damn good place to start.

Cuddled beneath the covers, Rhett kissed Corey's chin and then his neck. Corey closed his eyes and savored every sensation. With each brush of lips on his skin, Corey moved farther away from the horror of the day. Rhett was right. He saved Corey. Rhett was the one good thing keeping him afloat. He was so pure of heart. It wasn't charisma that drew people to Rhett. Rhett had an inner light that warmed the weary. He still believed there was good in the world. Corey had never believed that.

"Make love to me." The plea fell from Corey's lips without a qualm. He wasn't himself when he was with Rhett, and that was a good thing. Corey forgot to be on a mission. He got to simply exist with Rhett.

Rhett didn't say a word. He stole kisses while their clothes disappeared. All Corey could do was feel while Rhett's mouth explored his body. Corey's mind was quieter than it had ever been in his life. Rhett found his wallet where Corey put it on the bedside table. He never let Corey's skin cool, even as he rolled on a condom. His wet fingers toyed with Corey's asshole. Corey floated on a cloud. Nothing felt real. He knew he couldn't be hurt here in Rhett's arms.

A gasp stuttered from his throat as Rhett pushed his way inside. Then Rhett's tongue was in his mouth, and Corey forgot to think again. Rhett slowly rocked inside him, massaging him internally while stroking Corey's cock. Emotions and sensations mixed, fucking with Corey's head. He cared about Rhett. Corey didn't want to lose him. That was something Corey had never felt before. There had been no one he couldn't live without. He wasn't sure he could say that about Rhett.

"You're so beautiful," Rhett whispered between kisses. "The first time I saw you, you stunned me. Then I glimpsed your gorgeous soul and now I'm completely hooked." Rhett kissed him again, as if he couldn't bear to be without Corey's mouth, before tearing himself away again. "I've never felt the way I do with you. You're the first person I've met I don't want to live without."

Corey's heart skipped a beat. Rhett's words mirrored his thoughts so closely. They held each other's stare as the pressure built. Rhett's expression kept him captivated. Corey had never seen anything sexier. Rhett looked as if making love to Corey had him hotter than he had ever been in his life. Corey felt powerful. He focused his entire being on the moment. Corey needed to come, but he also wanted to watch Rhett fly apart. The moment it happened, an orgasm shook Corey's entire body. He swore his soul left him. Then Rhett's mouth covered his, and the pleasure doubled. Something powerful built in Corey's chest, changing him on a fundamental level. He knew he would never be the same after Rhett. So Corey had to find a way to keep him forever. There was no other choice.

CHAPTER SEVEN

HE WOKE UP ALONE. Daylight poured through the curtains, making Corey's gaze shoot toward the clock. It was noon and no one had woken him. He checked his phone. There were no missed calls or messages. A hint of disappointment wormed its way into his heart, even though he knew Rhett had to work. He wished Rhett had kissed him goodbye, at the very least. That way, his intrusive thoughts wouldn't get the best of him after the night they shared.

Corey rolled from the bed. He locked down his mind while he headed for the shower. All throughout his morning routine, he refused to think of anything except work. A care team should have arrived hours ago. If his patient was still alive, he would be much more comfortable today. Likely, Corey would need to keep him in a medically induced coma. Thoughts of his next steps carried him until he reached his medical wing. The full staff he requested had arrived, but that was not what had Corey drawing up short. Rhett was by the boy's bed, reading to him.

While fighting a smile, Corey accepted a chart of notes from a nurse and checked the vitals on the screen. Kid John Doe was holding on strong. Corey scratched some notes about medicine dosages before handing off the chart. He crossed the room and touched Rhett's shoulder.

Rhett started. He blushed as he looked Corey's way, as if embarrassed to get caught caring so much. "Hey. He probably can't hear me."

Corey couldn't let Rhett's kindness go unseen. "Some studies suggest he can. You didn't go to work."

Rhett shrugged. "This seemed more important, and I wanted to make sure you were left alone to sleep this morning. You're no use to anyone if you're dead on your feet."

Corey didn't know what to say. He was beyond moved. "Thank you." His gaze slid toward the bed. "How long have you been sitting here?"

Rhett checked his phone. "About two hours. His eyes opened for a second earlier."

Corey moved to check the IV. "That's probably not a good thing. If he wakes up in pain or panicking, his vitals could crash. He needs to sleep and heal."

When Rhett didn't speak, Corey turned. Rhett sat staring at the boy while chewing his bottom lip.

"What's wrong?"

Rhett's gaze moved his way at the question. "What'll happen to him now? I mean, is there someone out there looking for him?"

Corey grabbed his rolling stool and pulled it close. He sat and held Rhett's stare. It was funny how it didn't bother him to look directly at Rhett anymore. "There are people checking his DNA and whatnot, but likely not. A lot of these kids are born in what's known as breeding houses. Women are kept as nothing but basically brood mares.

They pump out children to feed the machine. It's rare for these operations to find kidnapping victims. Those are too high risk. They have people actively looking for them. That's not good for business."

Rhett's expression turned more crest-fallen by the second. "So, what? He'll go to an orphanage?"

He was sweet. Corey adored how much he cared. "The sponsor behind our group has a program set up for the kids we rescue. He'll go somewhere safe where he'll get the treatment he needs. That includes counseling and a good education. He'll thrive."

Rhett didn't look any happier. "So I'll never see him again or know if he's okay."

"Do you keep track of all your students?" Corey didn't want to sound heartless, but he didn't know any other comparison to draw from to help Rhett understand.

Rhett shook his head.

Corey nodded. "I can't keep track of all my patients. Occasionally, I'm lucky enough to see one again, but mostly, they move on to a productive future."

Rhett nodded. "I understand."

Corey couldn't stop watching Rhett. Rhett stroked the boy's arm and hair. He looked exactly like the mother hen Corey wished he'd had when he had been in the boy's position. Corey could love him. That thought sideswiped him. He honestly hadn't expected Rhett, but Corey could absolutely love him.

"Don't let them take him away until I know he'll live."

A smile exploded across Corey's face. Maybe he already did love him... just a little. "Don't worry. He's not going anywhere until I give the word."

Rhett's shoulders relaxed. He flashed Corey a sweet smile. "I guess I'm being ridiculous. I don't even know this kid."

Corey shook his head. "You're amazing."

They held each other's stare. Corey didn't know which of them moved first, but they met in the middle. Their lips brushed and then clung. For a moment, they simply shared each other's air. Corey wanted to keep him. For the first time, he wanted to be with someone more than he wanted his next breath. Rhett had to stay.

The day passed in a blur. Rhett knew he couldn't miss another day of work, but he also couldn't leave his new friend's bedside for long. Each time more than twenty minutes passed with him away from the medical wing, Rhett found himself rushing back. He felt protective and almost like a papa bear. Rhett had to see this through.

"He won't get better faster because you're watching him sleep."

Rhett cringed at Bear's words. Corey hadn't made him feel dumb for being here. But he got the impression Bear thought he was ridiculous. Unfortunately, Rhett was used to people thinking he was stupid, so Bear wasn't special. He knew what people thought of him. Rhett was that big, dumb jock who taught gym class because he was too much of an airhead to do anything else. Usually, he didn't let people's opinions bother him. It chaffed today.

"I disagree," Corey said, proving he was listening even though he sat quietly in the corner, studying charts. He finally looked up from his paperwork and focused on Bear. Corey didn't look inclined to hear any arguments. "What brings you by?"

Bear held up a file folder. "Got the kid's info. It's the usual stuff. He's just a number from a brood. No name. Russian born."

"He doesn't have a name?" Even Rhett heard the disbelief in his tone.

This time, when Bear looked his way, his expression screamed understanding. "It's just like that, doll. I'd like to say you get used to it, but you don't. You can name him if you'd like. I imagine Zander is running low on names anyhow."

Rhett's forehead furrowed. "Who's Zander?"

Bear glanced around and cleared his throat, sounding uncomfortable. "Anyhow." He passed the file to Corey. "I'm about to leave town, so I figured I'd hand deliver that and check on the boy one last time."

Corey nodded as he set aside the folder. "Thank you. He's hanging in there. I think he's holding on solely for Rhett. Otherwise, I can't explain how he's still breathing." They both looked his way, making Rhett's skin heat. He didn't usually mind being the center of attention, but this was different. Rhett felt exposed. Corey set him free by continuing his goodbye. "Have a safe trip home. Thank you for your help with the boy."

Bear nodded. "It's all part of the job." He glanced Rhett's way. "See you later, Rhett. You did good last night."

Another unexpected blush crept up Rhett's cheeks. People didn't usually compliment him on anything other than his looks. It was more uncomfortable than he expected. He mumbled some half-assed goodbye before going back to keeping his patient company.

Several minutes passed before words burst from Rhett without his permission. "Let's name him Rhorey. It's a combination of our names and it's also a fierce warrior in this video game I used to play."

Silence met his suggestion.

Rhett finally looked Corey's way.

Corey looked as if Rhett had struck him dumb. After a second, Corey visibly swallowed. "Um. I'm not sure you should pick a name right away. If he doesn't make it..."

Rhett made a dismissive motion, cutting Corey off. "He will. But for argument's sake, say the worst happens, he still deserves a name. We can't let him pass on nameless. He deserves to be more than a number."

Corey nodded. "Okay." Corey scribbled in Rhorey's chart. "Rhorey it is. We'll give him your last name."

Even though Rhorey Porter had a good ring to it, Rhett shook his head. "He should have your last name. You're a doctor. I'm just a gym teacher slash sometimes a visual sex worker. No one wants my last name."

Corey held his stare. He was getting good at that, and Rhett was getting addicted to it. "You're a wonderful man.

My doctor status doesn't make me special. Plus, no kid wants a last name no one can pronounce. It'll take him two years to learn to spell it."

Rhett bit his bottom lip. Corey sounded like he believed Rhorey would live. Not only that, but he also sounded like Rhorey would be part of their lives.

"What? What's that look about?"

Rhett shook his head. "Nothing. Porter it is." Corey didn't know it yet, but he had sealed his fate. Rhorey would get better, and Corey would keep them both. Rhett felt it in his gut. Corey was stuck with them.

CHAPTER EIGHT

Rhett: *What would you like for dinner? I'll pick it up on my way home.*

Rhett: *I meant your house. I don't know why I said home.*

Corey: *I knew what you meant. You don't have to get anything. I can cook.*

Rhett: *I know you can, but you shouldn't have to on top of everything else you do. I'll just pick something and surprise you.*

Corey: *Okay. See you soon.*

Corey: *Rhorey opened his eyes for a second today. Unfortunately, he immediately panicked, and I had to put him back under. I'm sorry he's not closer to getting better.*

Rhett: *He'll make it. I believe.*

Corey: *Would you mind stopping by the store on your way home?*

Corey: *I meant on the way to my house. You know what I mean.*

Rhett: *LOL! I get it. I may as well live with you now. The only time I go home is to grab more of my things. I think I have more stuff at your place than mine now. What do you need? I'll be happy to get whatever.*

Corey: *We're running low on canola oil.*

Rhett: *I'll grab it.*

Rhett: *I miss you and Rhorey. Today seems extra long.*

Corey: *So quit and come home. Just joking. I know you love your job.*

Rhett: *It's not the only thing I love.*

No matter how hard he cringed or over-thought things, Rhett couldn't unsend his final text to Corey. He was so damn close to admitting his feelings, but he didn't know how receptive Corey would be. Rhett thought Corey loved him too. They practically lived together now, but that was mostly because of life revolving around Rhorey. Rhett hadn't expected Rhorey to be in a medical coma this long. The longer he held on, the more Rhett couldn't quit on him. He was attached.

While waiting for Corey to respond to his text and internally freaking out, Rhett distracted himself by checking his website email. He hadn't checked it in forever. Hell, he had been losing subscribers in droves since he hadn't had time to upload any fresh videos. Rhett didn't have time for anything but Corey and Rhorey. It was a damn good thing it was the final Monday before school broke for the holidays. Maybe he would finally have time to make a few videos. He needed to make some money.

His jaw dropped as he logged into his email. The sheer volume of comments on his website form from people worrying over his health was astounding. An unfortunate number of them were from Marshall. That made Rhett uneasy. In fact, he'd had a bad feeling in his gut all day. Rhett didn't know if it was worrying over Rhorey not improving or if it was all in his head. Something just felt off. Rhett closed his email app without reading any of the messages. He couldn't deal with that now.

The landline on his desk rang.

Rhett eyed it. That line never rang. He answered, trying to sound as professional as possible. "Mr. Porter."

"Good afternoon, Mr. Porter. You're needed in Mr. Hargrove's office."

Rhett checked his watch. He only had fifteen minutes until time to leave and he wanted to get home to Corey. But it wasn't like he could say no to his boss, so his options were limited. "Of course. I'll be there momentarily."

Rhett disconnected the call and finished the last cold dregs of his coffee before heading out. He hoped he didn't have a problem with a parent again. There were an unfortunate number of parents who didn't think their kids needed to be subjected to the humiliation of physical education. Rhett didn't know why they thought he had any say in what was required by the state. That was teaching in a nutshell, though. He had enough power to listen to students and parents bitch but not enough authority to do anything about it.

His step slowed as he reached Hargrove's office. The door was open, so

Rhett poked his head inside. "You wanted to see me?"

Pete looked his way and waved him inside. "Rhett. Yeah. Come in and shut the door."

Damn. That didn't sound good, but Pete Hargrove had been the principal since Rhett started, so he didn't think they had a problem. He shut the door.

Pete motioned for Rhett to take a seat. He didn't wait until Rhett was fully in his chair before getting started. "We recently received an anonymous tip about a certain side job you've been doing. After a quick investigation, the claim has been substantiated."

Rhett's stomach dropped. Pete didn't give him time to defend himself, even though he didn't know what to say anyhow.

"Due to the immoral nature of your conduct, we've decided not to renew your contract next school year."

"Wait. What?"

"Furthermore," Pete said, talking over Rhett. "You'll be suspended for the remainder of the year, effective immediately. You can petition the school board for a reversal, of course. But in my opinion, that would be a waste of time. Not to mention, it would be extremely embarrassing for you and the school. Do you have any questions?"

It seemed like he should, but his chest and throat hurt too badly for him to think clearly. "No."

Pete nodded. "You have until the end of the week to clean out your office."

Rhett stood. There was nothing to say. He had always known this was a possibility. His contract had a morality clause. He had just hoped he could keep his tracks covered enough to keep him safe. Even knowing he faced the consequences of his own actions didn't stop the pains in his chest. He loved this job. Now it was gone. Not only that, but he likely wouldn't have any easy time getting hired anywhere else once word spread.

Rhett didn't bother going back to his desk. He had to get out of there. On his way to his SUV, he texted Corey.

Rhett: *Just got fired. On my way home now.*

He put his phone away and climbed behind the wheel of his vehicle. As he backed from his parking spot, he noticed Marshall heading his way. He looked crestfallen when Rhett didn't stop to talk. Rhett didn't doubt for a second exactly where that anonymous tip had come from. He didn't understand why Marshall had done it, though. Rhett drove to Corey's while his mind raced a mile a minute. First, he had to talk to Corey. While Corey had never voiced any opposition to Rhett's channel, Rhett didn't want to do anything that might harm their relationship. Right now, his channel was the only option Rhett saw as a source of income. He needed to get back to making content. In fact, he should probably hit Leather Bait and remind people he existed. With enough flirting and new videos, he could support himself full-time. At least, for a little while... until people got bored. Rhett wasn't getting any younger. He couldn't make these videos forever. Fuck. He was screwed.

By the time Rhett made it to Corey's, he had lost all hope. He might have to move to a different town if he wanted to teach again. Rhett didn't know how long his relationship with Corey would last if they never saw each other. Right now, Rhett stayed at Corey's every night, even when Corey went out of town, so they could see each other as much as possible. If they both worked elsewhere, they would never see each other. Rhett would never see Rhorey.

The house was quiet as Rhett came through the door. As always, he headed straight for Rhorey's room. Corey had moved Rhorey into a bedroom so he could have some peace. Rhett had slowly decorated the space for a kid. No one had said a word. Rhorey had full-time care so Corey and Rhett could work, but Rhett never stayed away for long. He knew in his heart Corey would wake Rhorey up one day and Rhorey would eventually get to be a real kid. When that day came, Rhett didn't know what he would do, especially if Corey sent Rhorey away. But Rhett knew Rhorey would get better.

As he stepped inside the room, he found Dante sitting quietly at Rhorey's bedside. Dante was the lanky blond who had helped save Rhorey's life the night he had been brought to Corey's. Since that night, Rhett had learned Dante had once been rescued by the secret team Corey worked for, but Rhett didn't know what Dante did for the team now, exactly. Sometimes, he got the impression he was better off not knowing a ton of details.

"Hey."

Dante glanced over his shoulder. "Hey. You're home early."

Rhett's throat swelled. "Yeah. Where's Corey?"

"He had to run out for a minute. I told him I'd stay until one of you got home." He checked his watch and stood. "Since you're here, I guess I should run."

"You don't need to leave on my account."

Dante shook his head. "I have a job tonight. So unfortunately—or hopefully, depending on how you look at things—you'll probably be seeing me later."

Rhett took a breath. Maybe he wasn't cut out for this life. He was already attached to Rhorey, and he never knew what would come through the door next. Rhett didn't know how Corey did this. "Okay. Be careful."

With a nod, Dante headed for the door.

Rhett didn't watch him go. Instead, he filled the seat Dante vacated and focused on Rhorey. He didn't want to think about the day or the future. Rhett let the worry over his imminent poverty fall away as he stared at Rhorey. Rhorey was so tiny and helpless. Rhett checked Rhorey's diaper and then the feeding tube in his stomach. He was getting good at being a nurse. It was strange how easily he had fallen into the role. He loved Rhorey even though they still hadn't officially met.

Rhett dropped back into his chair at the realization. Losing his job was by no means the worst thing that could happen to him. He didn't want to lose this kid. While Rhett couldn't even fathom the nightmare that had been Rhorey's life so far, and he also didn't know what sort of life Rhorey could expect now, Rhett wanted him. He knew Rhorey wasn't like a puppy or anything. Rhett couldn't decide to just keep him, but that was what he wanted. Unexpected tears welled in Rhett's eyes. He couldn't even afford to take care of himself now. How could he keep this child who would likely need expensive health care for the rest of his life? How could Rhett choose any other path?

The bedroom door opened, and Rhett swiped at his eyes. Corey stepped inside. He had a cake and balloons. Rhett blinked at the sight even as he came to his feet. "What's all this?"

Corey handed the cake and balloons to Rhett. "You had a bad day."

A bark of laughter burst from Rhett. "What?"

Corey shifted from foot to foot. "Cake and balloons make people happy, and you had a bad day."

The way Rhett couldn't stop smiling spoke volumes. Corey really knew him. He knew how to fix everything.

"Is it your birthday?"

Rhett jumped and spun at the tiny voice behind him. He nearly burst into tears at the sight of light blue eyes staring out at him from an angelic face. Rhett sniffed. "No. It's yours."

Rhorey blinked, looking confused and half asleep. "I don't have a birthday."

Rhett and Corey moved as one to the bed. "You do now."

Rhorey's gaze moved between them. "How old am I?"

Corey answered as he checked Rhorey's pulse. "You're six."

"Oh. That's a lot." Rhorey closed his eyes and rubbed his nose. "I'm sleepy."

Rhett fought back tears. "That's fine. You can go back to sleep."

Rhorey was immediately out again. Corey motioned with his head toward the door and Rhett followed. Once they were in the hallway, Rhett had to stop himself from jumping up and down in his excitement.

"He woke up."

Corey nodded. "I'd planned to tell you when you got home that I scaled back his meds. I think he's ready to start waking up a little at a time. Then I got your text. What happened at work?"

Rhett's excitement dimmed at the reminder. "They got an anonymous tip about my channel and suspended me for the remainder of the school year and will not be renewing my contract. In other words, I was basically fired on the spot." Rhett glanced down at the cake he held. It was covered in rainbows. A sad smile tugged at his lips. "I don't know what I'll do now. The only choice I have is to try to drum up subscribers and make a bunch of new content, but that won't last me forever." Rhett met Corey's stare. "And I don't want to hurt us, you know?"

"Why would that hurt us?"

Rhett shrugged. "I don't know. How long will it take before you get tired of that bullshit?"

Corey didn't respond right away, and Rhett recognized his silence, said it all. Rhett thought he might cry before Corey finally spoke. "Actually, when I got your text, I had one immediate thought. If you're interested in an alternative, that is."

"Of course." Even Rhett heard the desperation in his voice. He didn't want to lose Corey.

The way Corey suddenly couldn't look him in the eye again worried Rhett. "When I got your text..." Corey cringed. "As I'm saying it now, it sounds awful."

Rhett shot forward and kissed the corner of Corey's mouth. "There's nothing you could say that would make me think badly of you. You're amazing."

A small smile touched Corey's lips. Corey held his stare again. "The first thought I had when I saw your text was... good. You should be here with Rhorey and me. Full-time. This is your home. I think this is your calling. We need your help." Corey looked more vulnerable than he ever had. "I need you."

Rhett was scared to look too closely at things without clarification. "Are you asking me to move in with you? Or are you offering me a job? I'm sorry. I'm just confused. Is this about our relationship or my income?"

Corey made a helpless gesture. "Both, I suppose. You don't need your apartment. This is your home. I want you to be here with me because..."

"Because?" Rhett prompted, hoping against hope Corey would finally admit what they knew was the truth.

"Because I love you." Corey said the words the way he said most things; with little to no emotion. But his eyes were a different story and Rhett knew how to read him now. Corey feared rejection. That wasn't happening.

"I love you too."

"But?" Corey sounded sure Rhett was about to argue.

Rhett couldn't have that. "No buts. You're right. I'm supposed to be here with Rhorey and you." Rhett glanced at the cake again. For some reason, it gave him strength. Each time he looked at the brightly decorated confection, Rhett knew Corey was the one. He met Corey's stare again. "I expect a real job, though. Don't pretend I'm helping just so I don't feel bad about living on your dime. I really want to help."

"Don't worry. You'll always know your worth."

Damn. He couldn't believe this was happening. Rhett had wanted nothing as much. He started as a thought hit. "Oh shit. We have to get a tree and decorations and presents for Rhorey. We haven't decorated at all for Christmas." Rhett practically danced in place. They would have a real Christmas and Rhorey would have a real home. Corey hadn't said they could keep Rhorey yet, but he would. Corey was perfect like that. Their life together would be flawless. Rhett knew it in his heart. Corey never let him down.

Corey fought a smile as he watched Rhett turn into a giant kid. Once Corey set Rhett's mind at ease, ensuring him Rhorey wouldn't wake again tonight, Rhett was off and running. He wanted to do everything right then. Corey loved that Rhett immediately felt at home enough to search for a good spot for a Christmas tree. He just wasn't sure Rhett was being realistic when it came to the situation with Rhorey.

With his shoulder leaned against the wall, at the mouth of the living room, Corey watched Rhett rearrange some of the smaller furniture. He couldn't stay quiet. "A mental health team will be here in the morning for Rhorey."

Rhett froze. His gaze shot to Corey. "You're sending him away?"

The panic in Rhett's voice and expression had Corey rushing to explain. "No. They'll work with him here. I just want you to be prepared. Rhorey won't magically bounce from that bed tomorrow and be a normal kid. He has a tough road ahead of him on every front. You caring about him won't be enough."

Rhett smiled. "I know, but I'll still care about him, nonetheless."

Corey shook his head as Rhett immediately returned to his task. Truthfully, he had said all he could say, and he knew Rhett would still be Rhett. He was the giant over-enthusiastic puppy who saw the best in everything. Corey loved that about him. He didn't want Rhett to change. Corey just hoped reality didn't smack Rhett too hard over this.

"I'll make us dinner, then we'll go buy a tree." Corey turned away to do just what he claimed. He found one of Rhorey's nurses headed his way. Corey paused. His heart jumped into his throat. "Is everything okay?"

She smiled. "Yes. Rhorey says he didn't get his bedtime story."

Corey's gaze shot Rhett's way.

Rhett wore a huge smile. "I guess those studies were right."

Corey didn't know what to think. "It seems so."

Rhett headed for the hall. "I'd better read that bedtime story."

Corey shook his head and made his way to the kitchen. He had seen too many kids come and go. Corey knew the hell Rhorey faced. Yet he still let Rhett make him believe in miracles. Heartache lived down that road. Before he got the first vegetable cut, a rock-solid body pressed against his back. Corey sucked in a ragged breath. He swore his skin hummed in Rhett's arms.

Rhett's lips skimmed the shell of his ear. "He didn't last two pages."

Corey gripped the edge of the counter as Rhett's teeth sank into his neck. "I haven't completely stopped the meds. He's not ready for that."

Rhett's hand slipped beneath Corey's shirt. "He knew our names. He knows he's safe."

Corey couldn't focus on anything Rhett said. He was too busy feeling every touch. Rhett popped the button on Corey's pants. Corey tried to rally his thoughts. "I thought you wanted dinner so we could go get a tree."

Rhett chuckled against Corey's neck. "You bought me a cake for getting fired. Do you have any idea how amazing that is?"

Another stuttered breath escaped Corey.

Rhett's hand found its way inside Corey's pants. He massaged Corey's cock. "You're always putting me first and on a pedestal. You deserve to feel the same."

"I'm just glad you didn't fight me about moving here."

Rhett snagged Corey's jaw with his free hand and tilted Corey's head back. "I love you. You'll never have to twist my arm to be with you as much as possible." He claimed Corey's mouth. Their awkward position didn't matter. All Corey could think about was the hand on his dick. Rhett didn't tease. His pace had one goal. Whimpers rose in Corey's throat as he rode Rhett's palm. Rhett's kiss smothered the sound. Corey's balls drew up tight. He strained as he got closer to the edge. Corey quickly covered his erection with his shirt as his orgasm hit, keeping the mess contained. He cried out against Rhett's lips as Rhett kept stroking and drawing out every spasm. Their kiss turned sweet as Corey's breathing slowed. Everything felt right. Rhett would move in, and their life together would be perfect. They were in love, and that was more than Corey ever expected. If he could find this happiness, anyone could. Corey had never believed so much in fairytales as much as he did in that moment. Rhett made him believe anything was possible. They would get their miracle.

CHAPTER NINE

FOR THE SECOND WEEK in March, it was already hot as hell and Rhorey wasn't loving it. Rhett shifted from foot to foot while Rhorey silently cried against the side of his neck and stayed wrapped around him like an octopus. There was so much sweat between their bodies, Rhett wondered if he would have to wring out their shirts. They had only recently begun taking Rhorey places outside the house. He suffered from severe PTSD and got overwhelmed easily. That was why Rhett stood on the sidewalk outside the ice cream shop, waiting for Corey to handle their order. There were too many people inside. Everything was too loud. Rhorey needed a minute of quiet time.

He felt Rhorey go limp. A smile tugged at the corners of his mouth. Rhorey never lasted long once he started crying. He didn't have the energy to fight. Rhett kissed his temple and rubbed his back. He was tiny for his age because of the malnutrition and abuse. Rhett carried him way more than he should. Rhorey deserved to feel protected and cherished after everything he suffered. Rhett didn't think he could be spoiled at this point.

"Rhett?"

At the sound of his name, Rhett turned and nearly groaned aloud. Marshall headed his way. Rhett pasted on a fake smile but didn't speak. He didn't want to wake Rhorey, but fuck. He didn't understand how he had gone from not knowing this guy existed to seeing him everywhere he went.

Corey stepped outside with lemonade and a small cup of vanilla ice cream for Rhorey before Marshall closed the distance between them. Rhett nearly cried out in his relief. He did not want to deal with Marshall. It seemed like the man kept cropping up everywhere.

"All they had was lemonade."

Rhett flashed Corey a smile. "I'm sure that'll be fine."

Marshall's gaze moved between them as he made his way to Rhett's side, before landing on Corey. "Hi. I'm Marshall. My daughter used to be in Rhett's class."

Corey didn't spare Marshall a glance. "You take this," he said, holding the ice cream and lemonade out to Rhett, "and I'll take him. It looks like you need the break."

Rhorey barely stirred as he changed hands.

Rhett looked down at himself. Sweat molded his white t-shirt to his skin. He curled his nose at the sight before focusing on Marshall.

"Sorry. How is Terry?"

Marshall brightened the moment he had Rhett's attention. "She's good. She's with her mom this weekend. I know she's getting excited about graduating."

Rhorey sat up and looked around, blinking like he forgot where he was.

Rhett handed him the lemonade. "Take a drink of this, buddy. Then you can have your ice cream."

Rhorey nodded and took the lemonade from Rhett.

Marshall smiled in Rhorey's direction. "Who's this little guy?"

A deep line appeared between Corey's eyebrows. "This is Rhett's son and I'm his husband." Corey looked at Rhett. "Is this the guy who got you fired?"

Marshall's smile fell. "You got fired? I hadn't heard. Of course, I didn't do that."

Rhorey started crying at Marshall's loud tone.

Corey shot Marshall an annoyed look and moved farther down the sidewalk, talking quietly to Rhorey as he went.

Marshall watched them go. He looked genuinely upset. After a moment, he focused on Rhett again. "I swear I never said a word about what we discussed. Did they really fire you?"

Rhett shrugged. "They did, but it doesn't matter."

Marshall shook his head. "It does. You're a great teacher. You should be allowed to have a life outside of school. Is that why you shut down your channel? Would you like me to talk to someone? My cousin is on the school board, and I donate a lot of money to the sports program over there. I could twist some arms."

Rhett glanced behind him to check on his babies. Rhorey happily ate his ice cream while Corey pretended to steal bites. Rhett smiled at the sight. "Nah. I don't need the job. My husband is a doctor." He met Marshall's stare again. "I appreciate your willingness to speak up on my behalf, but I'm not interested in going back to a place where I'm not wanted. Plus, I'm enjoying being a stay-at-home dad."

Marshall nodded. His gaze slid toward Corey and Rhorey. "They're lucky to have you. When you told me you weren't single, I didn't realize you meant you were married. I'm still pissed you lost your job, though. That's not right. You were the only one who stood up for Terry. I'm sure you had a positive impact on other students too."

Rhett honestly appreciated the sentiment. He had loved his days of teaching. "Thank you."

A bright smile lit Marshall's face as he stared past Rhett toward Corey and Rhorey. "Some friendly, fatherly advice.

Make that kid walk. Otherwise, he'll have you carrying him everywhere until his feet drag the ground."

Rhett fought the urge to tell Marshall to mind his goddamn business. Instead, he smiled, nodded, and said his goodbyes before rushing to get to Corey.

Rhorey was already asleep again with ice cream covering his face and Corey's shirt. Even in his sleep, he held Corey's shirt in a death grip, as if he feared Corey might disappear if he let go. Rhett touched the small of Corey's back and steered him toward the car. He couldn't stop smiling while fighting the urge to dance in place.

Corey kept glancing his way. "Why are you smiling like that?"

Rhett shrugged. "You called Rhorey our son."

Corey didn't look the least bit guilty. "So? I also called you my husband. What of it?"

Rhett shrugged. "You being my husband is a given. I always knew we'd get married. But that's the first time you've admitted we're keeping Rhorey."

Corey's expression screamed confusion. "Of course, we're keeping Rhorey. I thought that was decided when we named him. Zander already sent the documents. He's been ours for months. Is that guy stalking you?" Corey asked before Rhett had time to recover from the news that Rhorey was really his kid.

"I don't know. It doesn't matter. What do you mean he's been ours for months? You didn't say a word."

Corey focused on Rhett. His heart was in his eyes, reminding Rhett of all the reasons he had fallen in love. "I didn't say a word because I thought you knew. There's nothing I wouldn't give you. Plus, he's ours. No one is taking him away or hurting him again."

Rhett bounced on his toes. He couldn't love Corey more. "We should get him a little tux and make him our ring bearer. How cute would that be?" The way Corey smiled and shook his head had Rhett fighting back a laugh. "Admit it. I make you tired."

Corey buckled Rhorey into his booster seat and closed the door. He didn't respond until they were in the car with the air blasting. He leaned his head back against the seat and held Rhett's stare. "You don't make me tired. You make me happy. Before I met you, I rarely smiled. Working was all I lived for, and that barely got me by. You're the best the thing that ever happened to me."

Rhorey snored.

A smile exploded across their faces.

Corey motioned toward the back seat. "That's the second-best thing. Let's get married."

Rhett's cheeks hurt. "I already agreed we would."

Corey held his stare, as if begging Rhett to hear him. "I mean now. Let's get married today."

Rhett's forehead furrowed. "There's a waiting period in Florida."

Corey shrugged. "We don't have to do it here. Rhorey is strong enough to fly. Let's just go and get this little family started."

"Okay." Rhett bit his bottom lip as soon as the agreement slipped out. His happiness was too much. "My mom will be pissed, though."

Corey put the car in reverse. "Call her and tell her to pack a bag."

Rhett stared at Corey as Corey backed from their parking space. He hadn't truly believed there was anyone out there for him like this. Then he had seen Corey in that bakery, and he hadn't looked away since. Rhett couldn't imagine any other life. His gaze moved to the backseat. Rhorey held his ice cream cup to his chest while he slept with his mouth wide open. Love made Rhett's eyes burn. Corey was right. They couldn't wait. He couldn't let this get away.

With his hands shoved in his pockets, Marshall watched Rhett leave. When Rhett had told him he wasn't single, Marshall hadn't pictured a husband and child at home. He didn't know why he cared. It wasn't like they knew each other. Marshall supposed it just seemed a bit odd for a guy with a porn channel to have a family. It bugged the fuck out of him that Rhett thought Marshall had gotten him fired. It made sense, of course. Marshall had approached him about subscribing to his channel, but damn. Marshall had said he wouldn't tell anyone. If a man couldn't keep his word, he wasn't worth the air he stole from the rest of the population.

"Are you stalking Rhett again? How embarrassing."

Marshall turned.

A lanky blond, probably no more than twenty, headed his way carrying two ice cream cones. "Excuse me?"

The boy smiled. He was definitely laughing at Marshall. He held the two ice cream cones out to Marshall. "Chocolate or vanilla? I'm not picky."

Marshall eyed the ice cream while wondering if he had lost his mind. "Did you just accuse me of stalking Rhett?"

A loud sigh met his question. "Take the chocolate. You don't strike me as bland."

"I don't want it."

Light green eyes rolled at his claim. "Look, it's hot and you'll be here a minute, explaining to me why you can't stop showing up everywhere Rhett does. So take the ice cream. I can't eat them both before they melt."

Marshall took the vanilla.

The blond smiled and licked the chocolate. "I'm Dante."

Marshall nodded. "Hey, Dante. No offense, but why are we having this odd conversation?"

Dante took a long lick of his ice cream cone while holding Marshall's stare. He looked wicked... like his name fit. Dante's eyes crinkled in the corners. "Eat your ice cream, Marshall."

Marshall took a bite of the vanilla.

A devilish deep rumble of laughter caressed his ears as Marshall ate. "Good boy. Now stay away from Rhett before I'm forced to make you disappear."

Marshall frowned. "Did you just threaten me?" There was no way this boy could take him in a fight. Marshall had nearly a foot in height and seventy-five pounds on the kid.

Dante shook his head. "I'm stating facts. Enjoy your day."

Marshall watched the kid, who was nearly as young as his daughter, walk away. He shook his head and tossed the rest of the ice cream cone in the trash. This town had gotten downright depressing. Maybe he would move away when Terry left for college. He was fucking sick of this place. No one nice lived here.

In matching tuxes, Rhett carried Rhorey down the aisle. Corey stood at the altar, waiting with his heart in his throat. They hadn't gotten here to this Vegas chapel as quickly as he liked. It ended up taking two days after everyone found out and wanted to come along. Corey realized now the wait had been worth it. All his friends sat in attendance along with Rhett's mom and extended family. Zander had sent his plane on more than one trip to get everyone here. Corey didn't see anyone but the man walking down the aisle, carrying their son.

They had gotten Rhorey in a tux, but there was no way he would walk down the aisle alone in front of so many people. His separation anxiety made day-to-day life a struggle. It was worth every second. Corey never expected this life or the love that choked him now. Rhett and Rhorey made waking up worthwhile. Before Rhett, Corey hadn't realized he had been just existing. Now he saw everything in a new light. He loved their life. Corey would die to keep it.

The way Rhett held his stare... damn. Corey's mouth watered at the ideas that look put in his head. He knew Rhett. Rhett planned to make their wedding night more than Corey could handle. Corey couldn't wait. When Rhett reached his side, Corey didn't hear a word from the officiator Zander hired. His emotions ruled all his senses. He had no clue how he found his voice to repeat his vows. Maybe he didn't. Corey had no clue what he promised. It didn't matter. Corey belonged to Rhett. Bubbly, over-the-top, and too much of everything, Rhett had really pulled the rug out from beneath Corey. He never saw this man coming. Yet he couldn't tell him no about anything.

"I now pronounce you partners for life. You may seal your future with a kiss."

Sound came roaring back to Corey at those words.

Rhett's smile turned wicked. He set Rhorey at his feet and snagged Corey's waist. Before he knew it, Corey was bent backward with Rhett's tongue in his mouth. The laughter and clapping from their guests had Corey fighting back a chuckle. Happiness filled him too full. He couldn't control the joy as it spilled over. Corey laughed against Rhett's lips.

"I love that sound," Rhett whispered for only Corey's ears as he righted Corey.

Corey hoped so, since he would likely be hearing the sound for the rest of his life. Together, they lifted Rhorey from the floor and headed down the aisle toward their new life as a family. Corey's face hurt from smiling.

"Daddy."

Corey glanced over to find Rhorey looking at him. His throat swelled. He never tired of that name. "Yes, baby."

"Can we have cake now?"

A bark of laughter burst from Rhett.

Corey couldn't stop smiling. "Only if you smash a piece in Dada's face first. Then you can have as much as you want."

Rhorey smiled and went back to clinging to Rhett's chest. "Okay."

Rhett slapped Corey's ass. "You'll pay for that one."

Corey hoped so. He hoped he spent the rest of his life being punished by Rhett. Corey couldn't think of a better way to grow old than spending it with his personal miracle. In fact, today seemed like the perfect time to get started.

Keep an eye out for the next Kings of the East, *Specialist*.

About the Author

Charity Parkerson is an award-winning and multi-published author with several companies. Born with no filter from her brain to her mouth, she decided to take this odd quirk and insert it in her characters.

*Eight-time Readers' Favorite Award Winner

*2015 Passionate Plume Award Finalist

*2013 Reviewers' Choice Award Winner

*2012 ARRA Finalist for Favorite Paranormal Romance

*Five-time winner of The Mistress of the Darkpath

Connect with her online:

*Sign up for her newsletter: https://sendfox.com/charityparkerson

*Join her readers' group on Facebook: http://bit.ly/CharitysTribe

*Website: https://www.charityparkerson.com

*A list of her social media accounts and giveaways all in one place: http://hy.page/charityparkerson

CONTENT

CONTENT WARNING: THIS SERIES is darker than my usual writing. Since these books bring back Zander and his fight against child trafficking, the deal in kidnapping, sex trafficking (along with everything entailed in that), suicide, and murder. A lot of these characters survived the worst things imaginable and now live with the scars. But now they fight to save people like them.

www.ingramcontent.com/pod-product-compliance
Lightning Source LLC
Chambersburg PA
CBHW060219180626
46813CB00007B/2887